THE
GURU

A Novel
By
Richard Hawley

ICARUS BOOKS

Copyright © 2011 Richard Hawley
All rights reserved.

SBN:0-615-48698-3
ISBN-13:978-0-615-48698-7

1

Andy-dam's Concern

Andy-dam closed the door of the Guru's sleeping suite quietly behind him and paused, troubled, in the tiled passage. Morning sunlight had barely irradiated the green ridges of the cay, but already Andy-dam could sense the oppressive force of the day's heat to come. Perhaps the Guru had felt this too, and this was part of his discomfort. More than discomfort, Andy-dam decided. There was a sadness, a kind of weariness and restlessness combined. The Guru was ill.

Andy-dam made his way to the sun parlor and was relieved to find the room bright and empty. Beyond the pier he could see the sun flashing whitely on the aquamarine. Andy-dam drew a cushion from the wall and seated himself to meditate. He must, he knew, recover the knowing and the steadiness he would need to address the seventy heart-sharers who had been granted their Life Retreat at Heart's Rest. This would be their third day, and while they had been dutiful and useful around the compound—and blessedly quiet—they had come for the Sharing, and this morning once again the Guru had declined.

Andy-dam's thoughts drifted to the ordeal, nearly ten years earlier, when the Guru had contended with hepatitis. It had begun, like this, with days of discontent and isolation. They were settled at the Star Shower compound near Aspen and were mid-way through the Spring Cycle of Sharings when the Guru withdrew. He had issued a printed Utterance that there was something deeply wrong—*toxic*, he had written—with the heart-states of the sharers, and he had asked for prayers and for a healing quiet. That delegation of sharers was then dismissed, saddened and hurt. The Guru remained in bed, listless and without appetite, even as another delegation of sharers arrived. Andy-dam had been surprised when the Guru agreed to meet them at the Arrival Feast. He had looked, to Andy-dam, drawn and without color, but he had been quietly kind to the guests. But as the Sharing proceeded into the Healing Sessions, the Guru abruptly withdrew again. The next morning he dictated on the mini-cassette recorder another Utterance which Andy-dam transcribed and distributed to the retreat delegation. *The toxicity is profound*, the Guru had written, *and it darkens the heart of the communion in its entirety.*

Even before the delegation could disperse, Elinore, then a heart-consort of the Guru's and also a physician, arranged on her own initiative to hire a car to transport the Beloved to a clinic in Denver. The Guru did not resist. Andy-dam had entered the Guru's chalet where Elinore, Maggie, another heart-consort, and Curtis Forbes were helping to gather the Guru's things. Andy-dam drew Elinore aside to ask her by what authority she had called for the car. He had asked her with prayerful affection and courtesy. He had taken Elinore's hands in his.

"He is very sick, Andy. He is passing blood."

"Passing blood?" Andy-dam had been startled—made stupid—by the phrase.

"In his urine. His urine is black, which means his liver is not working, and he is losing protein. Andy—he needs to be treated."

That spring and well into the summer, the posted Sharings had to be cancelled. Hospitalized for nearly two weeks in Denver after an allergic reaction to the first course of antibiotics, the Guru was quiet and very weak through most of the summer. With no revenue from the Sharings and diminishing reserves, it looked for a time that the Corporate Communion would be unable to meet its payments on the Star Shower Compound.

Andy-dam remembered that time as a mounting blackness, an accelerating descent. And then there was a saving Heart Beneficence from Curtis Forbes—the first check had been for seven hundred and fifty thousand dollars—and the slow but gladdening return of the Guru's health and Presence.

In August there had been the famous Augmented Sharing of Celebration. This was the Sharing of the Guru's Great

Laughter. Andy-dam remembered how the Guru had been sure again, and radiant.

Through the glass doors of the sun parlor, Andy-dam watched as Kamala, the Lasting Consort, greeted a pair of sharers as their paths came together on the grassy slope down to the pier. The guests, two slender women draped in brightly patterned sarongs, were embraced in turn by Kamala, then continued down the slope toward the shimmering sea.

Andy-dam felt the Peace in this. He would meditate now. He drew in a slow, deep breath and elevated his gaze over the retreating figures and the tapering pylons of the pier. He squinted out over the water to determine the horizon line, now an indistinct arc where dark water met the smoky blue atmosphere. Having found the horizon, Andy-dam relaxed his gaze, expelled his breath, and looked beyond.

2
Leaving Heart's Rest

In consultation with Kamala and Curtis Forbes, who had studied medicine but never practiced, Andy-dam proposed to the Beloved that an Entourage make arrangements at once to accompany him to the Cleveland Clinic where he could be thoroughly examined and treated if necessary.

As he listened to Andy-dam, the Guru, lying supine on his bed, felt a sickening spasm of discomfort in his scrotum, as if he were being gripped and cruelly squeezed.

"What is it?" Andy-dam asked, startled at the Guru's grimace.

For a moment the Guru did not answer, then he said, "It's pain." The Guru turned to Andy-dam, and Andy-dam could see the hint of humor, however weakly, in the Guru's eyes. "Mere pain, mere terrible pain."

"I'm sorry. Is there something I can do?"

The Guru grimaced again. He made a faint laugh. "Yes, Andy-dam. You can make it stop."

"That is my heart," said Andy-dam. "Let Kamala, Curtis, and me take you to the Cleveland Clinic. Curtis has made arrangements for you to see an excellent internist there, and a proctologist if necessary. Curtis believes the Cleveland Clinic is the best hospital in the world."

Again the Guru was smiling as he turned to Andy-dam. "Look out this window, and tell me exactly what you see."

Andy-dam looked out into the knife-blade leaves of the green palms as they shivered with the breeze from off shore. Through the palms, Andy-dam could see only bright sea and sky.

"I see palm branches and beyond that, the sea."

"And--?"

"And it lifts my heart. It makes me glad."

"And so, my friend, you want me to travel to Cleveland, Ohio, to visit a proctologist?" The Guru began a great heart-laugh, but the pain quieted him.

"Only until you are better. And besides," Andy-dam said with some urgency, "it is going to be hot here, too hot for your comfort. Come with us to Cleveland, get whatever is required, and we will go on to Star Shower to regain your strength. It will be cool and beautiful there."

"You are kind and thoughtful on my behalf." The Guru said. "If Curtis thinks this is necessary, we should probably go. He is usually right about the body. Another thing," the Guru continued, "This is a matter of the first chakra. The ugly—and also always honest! —heart of it all. Perhaps I am being told to come down to earth. Do you think?"

Andy-dam's heart suddenly swelled with a fullness and warmth he did not believe he could bear. The Beloved had once again, in heart friendship, asked of him.

"I would like to know what you think."

"You know," said the Guru, "That the first chakra is the cellar and furnace and first fountain of everything. In a sense, it *is* everything, except in its most vulgar, meaning its most honest, aspect."

Andy-dam said nothing. He hoped the Guru would continue.

"Do you know what this is like, Andy?"—*Andy, not Andy-dam*— "Let me tell you exactly. Let me speak as the first chakra speaks. Imagine a hand inserted somehow up between your balls and your anus. Imagine that hand up there squeezing the hell out of you. Are you picturing this, Andy? Feeling it?"

"Yes."

"Imagine also that you feel like shitting and peeing every second, even though you know it feels like passing fire even to try. Can you imagine?"

"Yes, and I am so sorry."

"That is the first chakra in a declaratory condition. And what is it declaring to me this morning? Is it come down, come down, come back to me? Is it saying, don't forget my power, my love? As if--"

The Guru fell quiet.

At length, Andy-dam said, "I'm afraid we must go in Meyer's little plane. The Kornbluth jet is away on company business.

"And Meyer's plane, no less," the Guru said weakly.

"Just to Nassau. The sky this morning is clear. It will be no more than forty-five minutes."

"Forty-five minutes in Meyer's plane..." The Guru said. He remembered vividly. The whine, the tinny chassis of the little prop plane seeming to want to spring its rivets at the terrible vibration, vibration that was unbearable on take-off and did not abate in the air. The Guru could hear it now. He could feel it in the fillings of his teeth. Another spasm. He could feel it in his contracted scrotum.

"Yes, I'll go," said the Guru. "One more hell. One more illusion. When we are ready, call the sharers together in the Session Hall. I will greet them and send them off. The Levinsons can structure a Quiet Retreat for those who want to stay."

"Very good—but are you strong enough for the Greeting. There are seventy of them."

"Of course I am not," said the Guru, "And of course I will."

3

The Educated Finger

Dr. Rana Sarinivasan, the specialist in proctology at the Cleveland Clinic selected by Curtis Forbes, confirmed that the Guru's prostate was indeed inflamed. But more worryingly, his manual examination revealed a hardened growth—"about the size of a pea"—protruding from the gland. "You can tell this," the Guru had asked, "Just by probing me?" The pain of the sudden intrusion from Dr. Sarinivasan's rubber-gloved hand had taken the Guru's breath away.

"In this peculiar specialty," Dr. Sarinivasan had said gently, "the educated finger can be a remarkably precise instrument. Now we must determine what kind of growth it is." That determination entailed, over the course of the following three days, a biopsy of the tumor, a colonoscopy, an irradiated enema, several scans, and blood work.

With Dr. Sarinivasan had reviewed the results; he told the Guru that there was a kind of cancer in the cells biopsied. The encouraging news, he added at once, was that this particular type of tumor was not known to metastasize quickly or unpredictably, indeed the other examinations revealed no signs of involvement.

"What is to be done?" The Guru asked.

"There are a number of approaches to consider. The most radical, the most conservative, would be to remove the prostate surgically. This would eliminate the cancer almost certainly—but there are likely losses of function you will want to consider seriously."

"That I will become a eunuch?" The Guru raised his eyebrows dramatically and smiled disconcertingly at Dr. Sarinivasan.

"There would be a loss of potency. Of course the least radical response would be to do nothing surgically, and to attempt to arrest any further growth with a course of medicines. Many men your age choose to do this and do very well."

"And continue to fuck!" The Guru raised a heart-laugh.

"And continue to have relations, yes. A middle course might be to try to shrink or even eliminate the growth with radiation."

The Guru, while not really looking away, seemed to absent himself from what Dr. Sarinivasan was saying.

Dr. Sarinivasan continued in a soothing voice: "As I said, there is much to consider, and you must take your time. Happily, we are not in a crisis. Your present discomfort should pass in a day or so as the medicines take effect. It is quite possible, you know, that this bout of prostatitis has nothing to do with the tumor. Bouts like this are common in men over fifty."

"So all of this highly technical buggery is actually ho-hum?"

"Excuse me?"

"It is nothing. And I mean that, sir. It is—all of it is—precisely nothing. For which I thank you. You have been wonderfully attentive to me and most kind. My medical advisor, Curtis Forbes, tells me you are a preeminence in your field."

Dr. Sarinivasan was startled by another explosive heart-laugh.

The Guru threw back his head and said, "The most educated of the educated fingers!"

4

"The Mystery of Pleasure"

The flight that would carry the Guru and his entourage to Denver and then Star Shower was delayed for several hours due to a faulty connection in the electrical system of the cabin. Andy-dam, with the Guru's consent, determined that they would pass the time in the non-denominational chapel of the Cleveland airport.

The Guru, feeling only a dull weight behind his scrotum but no pain, was now able to maintain a normal walking pace. His spirits, it seemed to Andy-dam and the others, were encouragingly restored. Nearing the open doors of the chapel, the Entourage had to maneuver around an obstructive line of travelers waiting to use the ATM machine. Andy-dam and Curtis stepped inside the chapel to look, then returned to where the Guru and Kamala were waiting and reported that the sanctuary was empty.

"Nobody in the chapel," the Guru exclaimed exuberantly, "and a waiting throng at the cash machine. Nowhere else in the world is there such freedom of worship."

Curtis made a smile of acknowledgement, but Andy-dam was concerned about the way some of the men in the ATM line were staring at the Guru. Vulgarly and intrusively, it seemed to Andy-dam, they were sizing up the Guru's magenta robe and the shiny golden straps of his sandals as one might ogle an attractive woman.

Seated together in a pew midway down the nave of the simple chapel, they passed a moment in silence contemplating the modernist panels of colored glass defining, had there been one, the altar.

"And this is God's house," said the Guru.

Andy-dam had begun to meditate when he felt the Guru's palm fall heavily on his shoulder.

"If you can locate your pad," the Guru said, "I would like to dictate a Teaching."

The Guru spoke, and Andy-dam transcribed in shorthand:

The Mystery of Pleasure is defined finally by its absence. And the absence of pleasure is not nothing. That is, the absence is not non-feeling. It is pain, discomfort, ache, cramps, searing, spasm, terrible weight where lightness belongs. Of course the Buddha emerged with this knowing as it applied to the entire human enterprise, as it applied to the whole desperate historical dance of temporal struggle. And it is the Buddha's perfect simplicity to enfold this roiling maya within the membrane of his infinite heart. And still no one wishes to learn! Jews, Arabs, Romans, and Greeks were so thickly concrete, so imperiously dense, that Christ had to paint a child's picture for them, a picture painted not with pigments on canvas, but with flesh and blood on earth, flesh and blood in the desert's heat, flesh and blood in a fetid river. Flesh and blood pierced by iron spikes, flesh and blood splayed on a cross. And still we turn away. And so we go. We go as if there were no dying, at least for us. We claim bewilderment at the eternal millions of sick and dying. We closet them in hospitals, where they are attended by the hopeless, evermore elaborate artifices of medicine and technology. The priests of medicine wear white gowns and green scrubs. They are busy as bees. They are awash in this abiding holocaust of pathology and dying. They are feverish to know more about it but resolutely refuse to know the one true lesson in their midst. This is a lesson any child can grasp easily. The only things that sicken and die are the things that CAN sicken and die. And so Christ said: See? See this? Here it is—excruciating death. And it is nothing! Christ died, and then, so that the thickest of the thick could know, said "here I am."

So this pain, this diminishing, this dying is precisely nothing. To suffer this is to shed a skin that was never skin. May we, as one in the great heart, shed that skin. It requires very little. It requires only to surrender and die. An unthinkable price? Consider then the reward. The reward is pleasure. REAL pleasure, heart pleasure. And, once again, the absence of pain and death is not nothing. It is not a void. It is communion with sheer, ecstatic being. It is to soar into the sigh of bliss.

This, my beloved, is the mystery of pleasure.

5

The Dream of Palatine

The Guru awakened suddenly, as if into another world.

His first, unclear impressions seemed to wash downward over his mind's eye like suds over glass: yellow fluorescence, the hum of air-conditioning, harsh rectangles of orange and green and yellow glass, dully illuminated from behind.

He sat upright. He felt a sickening weight, a sharp twinge somewhere between his spine and his bowel. He clasped his hands over the polished ridge of the wooden pew in front of him. Cleveland, he remembered. The airport, the chapel.

"Are you all right?" Andy-dam asked.

The Guru heard and did not hear Andy-dam's words. He blinked his eyes, not so much to clear his vision as to replace what he was seeing. The colored glass panels irritated him, and he felt something like anger arising.

"I am not quite here," the Guru said to Andy-dam without turning his head.

Something dull but persistent had occurred to the Guru while he slept. It had prevented him from descending into deep sleep. Indeed he had slept so lightly that he had the agitated and lately quite familiar impression of simultaneously being asleep and monitoring his sleep. He was aware of his head falling forward, the fleshy pressure where his chin collapsed into the folds of his neck. He had heard the snorts and gurgle of his troubled respiration.

He was aware in his dream state of trying to place himself. He had pictured a crude map, a child's map, in the center of which a large black circle, a void, was beckoning him. He knew this void was Cleveland. He might have been in a plane, but he also seemed to be disembodied consciousness ranging over the map face. He felt himself trying to locate Denver, to veer westward in that direction, but he could not do it. As he approached the black void of Cleveland, a similar void appeared to the west, and below it, in an inky typescript, the Guru read the word CHICAGO. The Guru felt only a mild resistance to veering left, toward the magnetic pull of Chicago's void. As he grew near, he felt an agitation in his body, felt his lips starting to mouth, "I know, I know."

"Are you feeling all right?" Andy-dam asked gently.

Listening to Andy-dam's words, the Guru could sense very clearly that the discomfort between his scrotum and the base of his spine was spherical. He could see it, and it was black, a void, as in his dream.

The guru turned to Andy-dam and smiled at him in a peculiar way. "Andy-dam, I am afraid I am going to cause problems."

"Problems?"

"Yes. I must change our plans. I have had a dream that tells me I must go to Chicago before we go to Denver."

Andy-dam looked bewildered, weary.

"I know it is awkward," said the Guru, "but I am certain."

"What will you do in Chicago?" Andy-dam spoke quietly, at the same time prayerfully seeking not to judge.

The Guru made a sudden exclamation of laughter—a throaty *hah!*—and said, "I don't fully know yet!"

The Guru pictured his father: his lean leathery face in expressionless repose, the wispy fringe of white hair around his clean baldness. The name of the town, Shaumberg, came back to him, where his father had entered the assisted-living facility after his stroke and his fall.

Andy-dam watched with fascination as the Guru receded within himself. He appeared, to Andy-dam, to be transported, unutterably happy.

The vision of his father's face worked as a kind of talisman, dissolving into a series of vivid images—vistas, rooms, storefronts, faces—of his boyhood in Palatine, Illinois. For the first time in weeks, the Guru felt light, playful, powerful. He could enter these rooms, cup those faces in his hands. Still smiling, the Guru closed his eyes and pictured the town library. There they were, Reference, Childrens, Science, Science Fiction. The varnished faces of the long drawers of the Card Catalog, A-L, M-Z. There was the sweet musty smell, the faint trace of gold leaf in the grooved spines. The Guru traced the block letters of RAY BRADBURY printed into the faded cloth binding.

"I will have Palatine back," said the Guru.

"I'm sorry?" Said Andy-dam.

The Guru opened his eyes. "I will go back to Palatine, where I grew up. It's northwest of Chicago. And I will see my father in Shaumberg."

"I better go to ticketing," Andy-dam said, rising from the pew and stretching. "Are you comfortable here? Would you prefer to be in the Club Lounge? We are members."

"I am a member of the Club Lounge?" The Guru gave another shout of laughter.

"Yes, we thought it would be comfortable when there are cancellations and delays."

The Guru could feel the weight again, the dull ache. "I will stay here." He looked around for Kamala and Curtis Forbes, but they had left the chapel. "You change the tickets and I will wait for you. And Andy-dam, in Chicago, I will need a car and driver for Palatine and Schaumberg. For the day."

I'll get to work," said Andy-dam, unsettled. The diversion to Chicago troubled him in a way he did not understand. He fought the urge to complain. He could see no end to the arrangements, and he knew already Curtis Forbes would make him aware of the added expense.

6
Sitting, Burning

———————

The Guru felt the terrible force of the ascending jet as a deliberate compression of his tender abdomen—as if two great hands were driving his guts back into his kidneys.

As the plane reached its cruising altitude, the pressure abated somewhat, but then the needle-point burning at the base of his scrotum resumed. Andy-dam had booked two first-class seats for his comfort, though the duration of the flight would be less than an hour. The Guru looked past the adjacent cushions to the oval window opening and saw the glass blue atmosphere receding to chalky mist over a thick mattress of white cloud. The sky, it seemed to the Guru, was a brilliant, infinite vault over a beckoning white bed. The roaring pellet of the plane, with its false, heavy stink, insulted the air. The Guru saw himself held captive by the plane's pretenses, as one of his boyhood heroes might be held hostage in an enemy spacecraft. *That would have been Flash Gordon.* The Guru smiled remembering the name. He said it aloud. *Flash Gordon.*

The stinging arose suddenly to a sharp spike of pain. The Guru lay his head back and made a barely audible hum.

Andy-dam and Curtis Forbes made their way forward from coach class to ask if he was all right.

"This imprisonment," said the Guru without opening his eyes, "is temporary."

"Would you like me to ask for some sparkling water, some juice?" Andy-dam said.

"More than temporary," the Guru continued, "It is actually an illusion. All we need" —the Guru opened his eyes—"is right outside the window."

Andy-dam could not think of anything to say.

"Care to join me?" the Guru said.

Andy-dam dropped to one knee beside the Guru's seat. "Since it will be mid-afternoon by the time we arrive and collect the bags, I think we should go directly to the hotel, which is close to the airport. There you can rest. We will have a light supper and relax. Then tomorrow morning, when you feel rested, the car can take you to Palatine and then to see your father."

"Thank you, Andy-dam. That is my exact wish."

Andy-dam felt a surge of steadiness, of strength.

"I will need the name and address of the facility where your father is staying. For the driver."

"It will come to me," said the Guru.

The Guru closed his eyes. He felt his conscious center descend from the region of his heart down into his distress, like a descent, it occurred to him, into a troubled soup.

The Guru pictured himself enveloping his inflammation as the atmosphere enveloped the groaning plane. In the picture he was brilliantly alight, weightless.

7

The Dream

The Guru could feel the dread, or fear, mounting as the cab stopped in front of the O'Hare Sheraton.

"Is this the place?" he asked Andy-dam.

"Yes. The airport Sheraton. Is it all right?"

The Guru chose not to disclose his foreboding. He was agitated but knew the hotel was not the cause. Stepping gingerly out of the car, the Guru straightened himself and stretched. The afternoon sky was grey-white, the color of the Sheraton. The newly poured concrete roadway which led to the Sheraton was lined in both directions with other chain hotels: Rooftop, Days Inn, Budgetel, Courtyard Marriott. There were no walkways, and the road itself was divided by a concrete median edged with a tubular white barrier. The facades of the other hotels looked to the Guru as if they were just out of walking range; nor could he see a way to reach one of them on foot, given the median barriers and the steady traffic through the wide intersections.

"This is not human," the Guru said, but not loudly enough for the others to hear. Before passing through the automatically open glass doors, he turned and looked back in the direction of the traffic. He wanted to see if there was a lawn, shrubbery, trees.

"Have you forgotten something?" Andy-dam called out from inside the hotel.

The Guru's agitated gaze fell, uncomprehending, on a strip of textured greenery tracing the oval of the drive. It might be grass, he knew, kept that unvarying shade of green by special chemicals. Or, he mused, it could be a synthetic surface, like the ones laid down in professional sports stadiums. He could not imagine people walking or lying on that grass. Aware that he should join the others, he lingered a moment longer. He thought there must be a tree or trees. He spotted a line of what were surely newly planted trees out beyond the hotel drive, running parallel to traffic. They were evenly spaced at intervals of several yards. The broom-handle trunks of each arose from dark cones of mulch, and they were held upright by barely visible supports of string or wire. *Not trees at all*, the Guru reflected, *not even continuous with trees.*

Waiting with the others at the registration counter, he formed, but did not share, an Equation: the living death outside the hotel was exactly equivalent to the living death inside the plane. Somehow, he knew, both were related to the warm, heavy, sickening ball below his belly.

Kamala noted that the little mound of rice, beans, and herbs was untouched on the Guru's plate. Setting aside the full glass of juice on the night table, she carried the tray back to the kitchenette.

When she returned with rolled washcloths, a pan of warm water and the oils, the Guru lay on his back on top of clean sheets. He had undressed, and a bath towel was spread loosely over the mound of his belly. The declining light of dusk was filtered by the bedroom's gauzy curtains, creating a soft, almost smoky atmosphere. Against the white sheets, the Guru's figure looked bronzed and dark. For an instant Kamala felt an impression of great peacefulness, a timeless beauty. It occurred to her with a breathtaking suddenness that the Guru might be dead.

"Beloved," the Guru said in a low, pleasing hum, "Are you here to wash me?"

"Yes," said Kamala softly. She arranged her things carefully on the night table. "Would you like me to turn on a light?"

"No," the Guru said, "the darkness is lovely."

The bed was king-size, and Kamala was periodically uncomfortable as she leaned over, first, to bathe and then massage the Guru with aromatic oil. Bending forward at the waist and bracing herself with one arm, she worked over the limbs and masses of the Guru's torso with long, slow strokes. To reach his forehead and scalp, Kamala had to incline herself to the extent that her face was poised just above his. She could feel the warmth of his respiration against her cheek. Twice her breast lightly grazed his chest. The Guru made his familiar low hum.

"Is there love in this?" the Guru asked.

Kamala paused to consider. "I believe there is. I know there is."

"I feel it."

Kamala stood at the foot of the bed, then bent forward again and began kneading the oil into the Guru's feet and calves. As her hands passed over his knees and on to the thick flesh of his thighs, the Guru felt a distinct twinge of arousal: a single heart-beat of glad expectation, followed by a clout of pain between his scrotum and rectum.

"Beloved," Kamala said, feeling the clenching of muscles above his knees, "are you all right? Is this too much?"

The Guru breathed deeply, feeling the pain disperse.

"Your touch is—just as it should be. But I am in a strange dialogue with pleasure. An argument!"

"Is there something you would like?"

"I have what I like, beloved. I have it. I have the peace of this dark evening, and I have your lovely hands. Blessed hands."

Kamala resumed working the oils, very lightly, into the Guru's thighs until the Guru clenched again. She lifted her hand away and stood up.

"That must be all tonight," the Guru said. "It would not be good to pleasure me."

Kamala moved to gather up the damp cloths and the oils. "Is there anything you would like?"

"Yes, beloved," the Guru said softly. "I would like to resolve this argument."

Kamala was confused.

"I would like to resolve it," the Guru said, "for eternity."

That night the Guru did not so much sleep as fall intermittently from consciousness. With each descent there was a vivid dream of Palatine. Together these dreams called him powerfully back to the town of his youth. Yet they also carried with them the emotional suggestion that he must return in order to be consumed and killed.

He was swept into the old neighborhood over the shimmering green tops of the elms. Like a hovering bird, he felt himself deliciously suspended in the summer air, peering down at the smiling façade of the house at 174 West Walnut. The view of the house—its grey clapboards and darker grey trim, the bright blue door, the irregular red paving stones his father and he had put in between the front porch and the street—made him want to shout with pleasure. Then he began a slow descent to street level, and the atmosphere grew charged and heavy. Overhung with elms, the shady lawn and the beds of impatiens flanking the front steps were pungent with damp earth. Gnats clustered along the hedge, wasps looped and bumped metallically against the shutters. It was his house, the real house at 174. *It held the secrets*—again there was an impulse to cry out in exuberance—but something else was emerging, something cumbersome, threatening and heavy in the air. There was a dampness, a dankness in the shade. It penetrated the house, and the grey paint was now heavy with moisture, somehow breathing under its weight, breathing with terrible difficulty.

Now the Guru was disembodied, pure consciousness, and he proceeded into the house. The little vestibule inside the front door was airless. The closet door stood ajar, and the winter coats were swollen with summer heat. There was the kitchen smell, newly disturbing, faintly foul like an old dog, the stale redolence of steamed broccoli, butter long melted in its ceramic trough. His father's green chair loomed forward enormously, a stained orb where his head would meet the upholstery. There was the familiar ring marring the surface of the lamp table, powdery ash in the oily tracks at the bottom of the ash tray, untidy sections of the *Tribune* piled up next to the cork bottomed coasters and the *TV Guide*. In the dining room, too, there was positively no air, and the Guru could sense a punishing dry heat emanating from everything. The mullions of the dining room window framed separate shafts of dust motes, and a creamy dust was part of the fabric of the lace tablecloth. There could be no breathing in this room, and to proceed into the dark kitchen—the Guru could see the faint gleam of the Formica tabletop—would be to succumb to the abyss. Utterly airless, the house would suffocate him, dry him to powdery dust.

Back outside now and up to the tips of the leafy elms, and air—the Guru, through his sleep, was aware of his own labored gasping snores. He could not go back there. He must ascend, up and into the good air, but the secrets were down below, caught in the house. The bears were pawing the rear window, and the Guru could see a flash of sunlight glinting off of Granny Mueller's glasses as they were huddled together in the front seat of the Ford at the Lake Kroehler dump. The Guru felt, as he had long ago, mortally exposed and wonderfully safe at Granny Mueller's side in the front seat. *He would live.* "You're a big boy today, Harris," Granny Mueller was saying. "You're my big boy today," and now he was again finishing The Great Swim, and his lungs were stinging and his arms were leaden, but he would will the last few strokes, even if he was practically slapping the water, it would take to reach the ladder at Norton's Float. The Guru could no longer see Granny Mueller or sense her presence, but he heard her voice, as he staggered, shivering, knees wobbling, up the ladder of the Float. "You *did* it, Harris. You did it. You're my champion."

Champion.

The Guru descended into deepest sleep.

II

The Guru Goes Home

1

West Walnut

Outside the entrance of the Sheraton, Andy-dam reviewed the day's itinerary with the driver, Forrester, who seemed familiar with the northwest suburbs. When the Guru emerged on the pavement, flanked by Kamala and Curtis Forbes, Andy-dam thought he saw Forrester start. The Guru, especially in contrast to Curtis in his casual travel clothes and Kamala whose pale green sarong could pass for an ordinary summer dress, stood out strikingly on the walkway. He wore a robe of deep rose red, and his golden medallion—the Sanskrit symbol for birth—flashed brightly in the morning sun. The light had already clouded the Guru's prescription sunglasses to the extent that his eyes were unreadable. With some concern Andy-dam noticed that the Guru's great head and the flesh of his arms looked strangely colorless, almost grey.

"So, Mr. Forrester," the Guru said when he had been introduced, "You are my driver and guide into the past."

"Yes, sir," said Forrester uncertainly, looking down at his neatly printed instructions. "Palatine, 174 West Walnut, then to Schaumberg to Villa Serena Assisted Living, then back to the Sheraton."

"Excellent," said the Guru quite loudly. "And this is our craft—a Lincoln *town car*. Excellent. Off we go."

Andy-dam held open the door to the back seat. When the Guru was seated and comfortable, Andy-dam leaned inside and said, "We will be waiting for you. Should we expect you—when— late afternoon?"

"Yes," said the Guru, almost shouting. "Expect me then. Andy-dam, you must expect me always."

Andy-dam looked hard into the browned lenses of Guru's glasses. "We will be right here."

The Guru too had noted Forrester's wariness as they greeted one another, and he was relieved. Forrester had addressed him as *sir*. This was good. There would be no wearying chat, no unbearable chumminess. He was glad that he had declined Andy-dam's and Kamala's company. It was good to sit back in the air-conditioned hush of the dark car. It was, the Guru felt, more restorative than sleep.

Some time after their departure—it seemed to the Guru quite a while—Forrester, stopped at a light, slid back the glass panel separating front and back seats and said, "We can take the toll road all the way out to the race track in Arlington, but the season's started, and it will be busy today, or we can go in on 14. Do you have a preference?"

"No." The Guru let out a harsh laugh. "Absolutely none."

The Guru did not so much recognize as feel greedily gathered in by the familiar streets beyond the tangled hub of Palatine's commercial district. As the town car approached West Walnut on Flaherty, the Guru tapped the glass partition with his finger nails.

Forrester pulled over to the curb.

"The house is over there, at the corner of the intersection. I would like you to pull forward a little and stop the car. I would like to look at the house for a while."

"You want me to stop here? I could pull in front of the residence."

"No. I want you to stop here, just ahead. Just as I told you."

Forrester pulled up toward the intersection and stopped. He looked into the rear view mirror for a sign from the Guru but could read nothing behind the cloudy lenses.

The Guru leaned close to the door and peered across the street to the shaded lawn and dappled façade of the house. The hedge that had lined the sidewalk had been removed, which made the low-slung bungalow look exposed and somehow vulnerable.

Subsequent owners had retained, or perhaps not bothered to repaint, the grey and darker grey of clapboard and shutters. Something else, harder to define, conveyed an impression of indifference and neglect. The lawn, not necessarily overgrown, showed irregular sprays of crab grass, the odd spent dandelion stalk. There was something else—then the Guru saw it. The gutters were in disrepair. Even from across the intersection he could see that they were bowed and mossily discolored. Here and there a seedling shot up from the overflowing packed leaves.

The Guru felt a flash of anger, then let it subside. *Yes*, he said to himself, *they have let it go.* The realization began to please him. *Of course they have let it go. Its genius has passed.*

Genius. The Guru let the tears well and stream down his cheeks.

Again the glass panel between the seats was chafing in its track.

"Should I just—stay here?" asked Forrester.

"Yes," said the Guru sharply. "I would like to stay here, *quietly.*"

2

The Summer Without Air

The Guru rested his forehead against the cool window glass of the Town Car, and it occurred to him that it made him feel like a spy or a burglar or an assassin to be peering out at the grey house for such a long time. The thought made him smile.

He pictured himself as he had been, the seven-year-old boy in jeans rolled up at the cuffs, a striped tee shirt. In the shiny Kodak snapshot he stood in profile, staring alertly at the sausages and patties beginning to sizzle on the outdoor grill in the back yard. There he had been, in that yard, in that family, at that time. He had been seven. 1950.

Very specifically, very completely, he had been Harris Mueller, son of Otto and Dot Mueller. It felt strange to the Guru to call up his mother's name. He associated the grey house almost entirely with Granny Mueller, whose house it had originally been and into which Harris and his father moved after his mother's decisive yet, for the Guru, not quite real death in the aftermath of an asthma attack as the family was returning from a Sunday picnic at Fox

Lake. His father had been at the wheel, his mother, still in her swim suit, in the passenger seat. He and Granny Mueller were in back, separated by the wicker hamper. The Ford had been stifling, and his mother had opened the vent and rolled down the passenger seat window. Not long afterward she began to make a wheezing sound, then very deep, labored breaths which trailed off, in the Guru's memory, into a kind of whistle. "Otto," she had said, turning to her husband with a desperate, frightened look, "*Otto*, I need help." Then she pitched forward, and the Guru could only hear her bronchial honks and gasps. They pulled over into the lot of a seasonal eatery called Chicken 'n a Basket. His father went inside to telephone for help, and Granny Mueller moved to the front seat to tend his mother. It took a long time for his father to come back to the car, and the Guru could remember the prickly heat in his face. Through the open car windows he had smelled the salty sweetness of french fries and chicken from the restaurant grill. It made him very hungry, but no meal was offered, not there in the lot or later at Northwest Community Hospital or that night at Granny Mueller's house in Palatine, where he was told he would stay until "the services." He had not asked what the services were but sensed they would be profound. It was a treat to stay at Granny Mueller's because she was slow and warm and kind, and she kept a china bowl of M & Ms on the coffee table. But that night Granny Mueller's face had fallen slack, drained of all energy. She had made the Guru cry. Kneeling at his bedside, she told him, "We've lost your mother." He wondered how she could have been lost. He pictured the firemen wrenching his mother from the Ford. They had stretched her out on her back in the parking lot when Granny Mueller led him away. He had not wanted the firemen to see her like that in her swimming suit, to see her big arms and legs. He could not see how she could have been lost there or in the ambulance or in the hospital.

The Guru recalled feeling unreachably separate, irrevocably singled out to have lost his mother. It was the beginning of a powerful separateness to come, an avatar, he would come to understand, of his God-self, revealed years later in his Utterance on Importance.

The Guru felt a dull but insistent ache behind his scrotum, and he shifted his weight. He stared again at the grey house across the intersection. Slightly unkempt, dampness mottling the concrete of the front stoop, the bungalow seemed settled on its foundation, but hardly substantial. *It is perfectly unimpressive*, he said quietly to himself. Then the Guru was visited by a flurry of images and recollections.

3

The Flat Ginger Ale

That summer he was held suspended in the dry, airless atmosphere of Granny Mueller's living room. After breakfast, they did the dishes together. It was his job to wipe them dry when she set them down in the dish rack. The dark plastic radio, set almost inaudibly low, emitted muted passages of the tunes of the day. After a few days, he had committed some of them to memory.

Are you warm, are you real, Mona Lisa

Or just a cold and lonely lovely work of art.

And:

Lonely rivers flow to the sea, to the sea,

I'll be coming home, wait for me.

After breakfast Granny Mueller would leave the house and walk into town to her shift at the bakery. Between breakfast and her lunch break and then after lunch until four, he was to play in the house or in the yard, but nowhere else, except at the Kendalls' next door where he could play with their younger boy, Buzz. Granny Mueller had brought Mrs. Kendall and Buzz into the house to meet him. Buzz had said *hi* tersely. He looked older and was much taller. Buzz seemed uncomfortable, even annoyed, to be standing next to his mother in Granny Mueller's kitchen.

The first morning alone he had walked from one end of the house of the other, quietly searching every room, opening every cabinet, every drawer. In Granny Mueller's bedroom desk he had found a polished silver dagger in a green leather sheath, which he slid under his belt. That evening she told him it was a letter opener and that he must leave it in the drawer.

On the second and third mornings he had paced and searched the house but found everything exactly as it had been. This had made him feel desperate and frightened in a new way, and he felt as if he was going to cry. He remembered Buzz Kendall from the kitchen and went next door and tapped his fist on the back door screen. At first no one came, but then a figure, Buzz, made his way through the darkness inside to the other side of the screen door.

"Hi. What do you want?" Buzz Kendall said.

He did not know. He wanted to run back across the yard. Then he said. "Do you want to play?"

"Play what?"

He felt paralyzed. He did not know what to play.

"Play what?" Buzz Kendall said again.

"My grandmother has a dagger in her desk."

"What about it?"

Buzz Kendall was not being nice. The Guru bowed his head. Again he thought he would start to cry. Buzz Kendall stepped back from the screen and closed the kitchen door.

He was allowed to watch television. There were shows for children in the morning in which clowns talked and sang in an exaggerated way to children in the same bright room. There was a cowboy who talked to a boy puppet who sat on the cowboy's lap. One of the shows was a circus, but it took place very morning in the same small room. A clown told stories, and pictures from the stories appeared on the screen. He found the stories, like the shows themselves, slow and overly obvious. The children who visited the television circus were younger than he was. He found himself waiting impatiently for the moment when the clown would pick a boy and a girl to reach into a giant jar of pennies and pull out all they could hold onto.

When Granny Mueller returned to the bakery after lunch, there was often a baseball game on channel nine. There was an elusive energy to the baseball broadcasts that compelled him to watch and listen, although the games themselves were to him agonizingly slow, most of the figures nearly inert. The pitchers waited tantalizingly, intolerably between pitches, and sometimes, when they seemed ready to throw, the batter would step away from his place.

He had learned the language of the baseball. Foul balls, the endless foul balls. Four balls, three strikes. Fly ball. Base hit. Homer. Home-run. Extra bases. Fielder's choice. That summer he had learned to measure time in innings. Two or three innings could make an hour, and by eight or nine innings Granny Mueller would be home.

Baseball had felt like a perfect contradiction, a contradiction he could feel in his restless arms and legs. So little *happened* in the baseball game, yet the announcers' voices were lively, on edge. The roar and whoosh of the stadium voices sounded to him like ominous winds rising and falling, like the arrival of exciting waves at the Waukegon dunes. In baseball, something exciting—like a homer—seemed always just on the brink, but almost never realized. Even now, sitting in the Town Car recalling it, the Guru could feel the heavy tedium in his legs and bottom as he readjusted his reclining posture on the living room floor in front of Granny Mueller's Zenith. At supper she would pretend to scold him for finishing so many of her M & Ms and Pepsis. "You will have no appetite for supper."

To his surprise and to his pleasure, he found that he could drink Pepsis endlessly. The deep, full sweetness on his tongue, arriving fizzily through the carbonation, was a renewable comfort.

After a few weeks Granny Mueller had taken pains to hide the Pepsi cartons somewhere, leaving just one behind for him in the refrigerator. But even trying to savor it, a Pepsi could not take him through one inning.

It was during the Baseball summer that the Guru had begun to experience the Signs—and to realize they were often terrible. He was lying on the carpet before the Zenith, Cubs and the Philadelphia Phillies. Only a few innings had passed, and he stretched his legs and wriggled with discomfort. He had finished the Pepsi, but the last syrupy taste still played pleasingly in his mouth. He went to the refrigerator in search of another, perhaps left about carelessly. There was only the half gallon bottle of milk, moisture beaded on the glass, an egg carton, bottled pickles, the bowl of yesterday's cole slaw covered with foil. Without expectation, he looked over the pantry shelves, the cupboards under the counter. Then he saw something. Below the towel rack in the dark recess between the counter and the refrigerator, he could see the dull gleam of bottle tops in their carton. Clearing away the stack of empty shopping bags, he recognized the soft drink carton and pulled it out. But it was Canada Dry ginger ale. The bottles were empty except for one still capped. He pulled it out and saw that it was half full. He looked for the can opener but found he could pry off the loose cap with his thumb. The dirty yellow beverage was warm and only faintly sweet on his tongue. There was something watery, almost soapy in the taste. He had heard the word before, from his father: *flat*.

He took the bottle into the living room and sat down in front of the TV. In his memory, he had been slightly stupefied, unseeing as he finished off the warm ginger ale in slow sips. When the last of it would not seem to come out, he held the bottle up to the window light to see what the obstruction was. It was a centipede, magnified vividly and horribly by the thick green-tinted glass. He felt a tingling grip at the back of his neck. The sunlight passed through the translucent carcass of the centipede, which seemed to glow with importance. *Poison*, the word more than a thought, came to his mind. But he knew he had not been poisoned. He had, rather, encountered sheer awfulness. He felt awash in it, as the centipede was awash in the stale ginger ale. He had touched the papery tickle of it with the tip of his tongue.

4
The Fixed Tiles

Down the back hall in Granny Mueller's bathroom he would sit on the toilet for a long time, even if he barely had to go. The bathroom was a hushed haven from the hiss and crackle of baseball. He would not turn on the light. The floor beyond his sneakers was tiled with small cream-colored rectangular pieces, some of which were about the length and width of his thumb, others the same length but twice as wide. The wider tiles were fitted perpendicularly to the slender ones and seemed to cap them, as he liked to cap the posts of his building block doorways with a heavy lintel. The tile triads—the slender pairs and wide caps—were themselves set perpendicularly to one another, creating a lively mosaic effect which, when he learned to relax his eyes, seemed to vibrate busily before him. By readjusting his gaze, he could still the vibration, and in time he learned to see the grid as a maze through which he could trace serrated trajectories in any direction.

The tile floor of the back bathroom had presented the first Pattern. He had written exhaustively on the meaning of the Patterns in the Utterances published together as *Simplicity in Complexity.*

The Guru concentrated then relaxed his gaze on the grey façade of the house across the intersection. It was as if the walls had disappeared or become transparent. He could penetrate the ell of the living room, move noiselessly down past the kitchen to the back bathroom, lose himself again in the fixed pattern of the tiles.

5

The Wading Pool

Not that first summer but the next, when he was eight, Granny Mueller arranged that he would go with the Kendalls to the park district swimming program. In the mornings there were scheduled lessons, conducted in ability groups. In the afternoon there was, upon presentation of a pass, free swimming in the Big Pool, Intermediate Pool, and Wading Pool.

He had dreaded the morning lessons with an intensity that sometimes made him sick to his stomach. The mornings were frequently overcast and chilly, and the dew on the grass felt icy and wrong between the straps of his sandals. Mrs. Kendall greeted him cheerfully and sometimes would address a question to him in the car on the way to the park, but Buzz and his older sisters rarely spoke to him.

Because he could not swim, he was grouped with the Tadpoles, who were further divided into floaters and non-floaters. The floaters progressed into Minnows, who could swim—kick, stroke, take breaths—but not yet swim across the pool. When a child could swim two widths of the Big Pool, he or she became a Fish. With the mastery of other strokes and dives, one became a Flying Fish. Beyond Flying Fish was Life Saving or Swim Team. Buzz was a Flying Fish. The girls were on Swim Team.

He was placed in the Tadpoles, a non-floater. He felt the weight, the apartness of being the oldest and tallest of the Tadpoles, some of whom could not touch bottom at the three feet end without gripping the drain ledge for support. Being so big and, he felt, calm among the gasping, goose-pimpled younger children made him watchful. Gwen, his teacher, regarded him with special warmth. She was Swim Team, and he was fascinated by the matted tangle of mercurochrome-colored hair visible below the line of her bathing cap.

"Today is the day, Harris," she would say brightly.

"We'll see," he would answer, opening his eyes wide to her in his Owl aspect.

He learned to hold his breath and to bow his face down and blow bubbles into the cold water. Gwen had helped him to extend his arms before him as he did this.

"That's it, Harris. That's almost it. All you have to do now is fall forward. Lift up those feet and glide away."

"I don't want to glide away," he had said, but he did not mean it. Especially when the sun was bright overhead, he longed to glide away on the surface of the sparkling aquamarine. Yet it would mean giving up something indescribably important and secure. He was both reassured and discouraged to see his feet firmly planted on the blue-green pool bottom. It would be a loss, a surrender, to give up his footing.

"There you go, *there* you go," Gwen was practically shouting at one of the littlest Tadpoles who was suspended prone over the water's surface, excitedly thrashing his arms and legs, floating.

The Guru's feet and legs grew heavy, rooted to the pool bottom. He felt something familiar—the arrival of tears, shame—mount in his belly, and he bowed his head into the water and blew bubbles.

The breakthrough had come in the Wading Pool which, though used only by the smallest children—babies—and their mothers, he preferred to the noisy horseplay of the boys in the Intermediate Pool.

He liked the Wading Pool, liked coming to rest in the soupy warmth of its shallows, the cheerful pale green of the water under bright sun. Sometimes one of the toddlers nearby would seek him out to play, wordlessly offering a glistening pail or an inflated plastic ring. Periodically a curious mother, observing his solitary scuttling or bellying over the pool bottom, would approach and ask, "Are you here with your mother? Your brothers and sisters?"

"No," he had learned to say, "I am waiting."

By July the afternoon sun on a clear day created a dry insistent pressure on his skin, and sometimes, unless he was in the water, the blast of heat from the concrete pool deck made it hard for him to breathe. On those days he liked to sit back in the shallows a few feet from the pool's edge, leaning back on his elbows. Once, when his arms could bear the strain no longer, he rolled over on his stomach and realized that, except for his forearms' intermittent contact with the pool bottom, he was floating. He felt a surge of excitement below his heart, a ringing in his ears. *I will test it*, he said to himself. He dipped his face into the warm water and blew bubbles. He opened his eyes and saw shimmery diamonds of light on the pool bottom just inches before his face. He raised his arms from the pool floor, and felt himself suspended in the gentle warmth. *Floating*. It felt like an ascent, as if he were held, caressed in a delicious medium neither water nor air, and his smile radiated not just along his jaw, but down his spine, splaying out ecstatically through his belly, groin, and down the backs of his legs. The ripples of green water just beyond his ears made little sighing, plopping sounds: *dap, plip, dap*. The chattering of the children and the mother's poolside babble were in his ears, yet worlds away. He moved to the center of the Wading Pool, where the water was above his knees. He knelt down, held his breath and, again, sent himself gliding over the water's surface. There had been instants before, shards of it, certain tastes on the tongue, a play of light on the bedspread in the morning or on the lawn—but here it was, sustained and, he knew, renewable at his will. *Yes, yes, yes,* it had always been around and about, hovering, atmospheric, but here it was, coherent and all at once: *happiness.*

6

The Great Swim

It made the Guru smile again to re-embody his floating. The images of sun-dappled water carried him to other waters, other pools, the brown water of rivers, the honey colored stones speckling the bottom of Lake Kroehler.

Granny Mueller had taken him, when he was ten, for two weeks in August on Michigan's Lower Peninsula. She had somehow identified and arranged to rent a cottage at Spruce Lodge on Lake Kroehler. They had spent a full day, from early morning till sunset, driving north in the Ford. His father would drive up to join them the second week.

"It will be an adventure," Granny Mueller said.

Passing first the manure-pungent dairy farms, then stretches of thick pine woods, the Guru had wondered what the adventure would be, how it would arrive.

At midday, they stopped for frankfurters and french fries at a weathered roadside restaurant called the Teepee. Over their table, a shiny brown coil of sticky paper, dotted with flies, swayed in the draft of the window fan. They carried their paper plates outside, into what Granny Mueller called "the fresh air." Seated at the weathered picnic table near the road, he was uncomfortably aware of cars passing behind him at high speed. It gave him a frightened feeling in his mid-section, and with each whooshing pass, he felt as if something was being sifted out of him.

When Granny Mueller went inside to pay the bill, he was aware of an argument erupting behind him. A man with black shiny hair and sleeves cut away from his tee shirt rose abruptly from his seat and started stuffing the food in front of him into a paper bag. The woman sitting opposite, who had a hooked nose and pitted cheeks, started to cry.

"Go ahead, you son of a bitch," she said, "go ahead!"

"What did you say? What did you call me?"

The Guru felt the air around him shatter like glass.

"You're a son of a bitch. I called you a son of a *bitch!*"

The man with the oily hair pushed the bag of food into the crying woman's face. With his other hand he slapped her loudly and hard. She rose shrieking and flailing her arms at the man. Her nose was bleeding. From behind the restaurant screens a man's voice shouted, "You cut that out. You get outta here. I'm callin' the cops."

As Granny Mueller stepped outside, the man yanked the woman's wrist and led her up into the cab of the truck. He returned to the table for his food, and the Guru could hear the hollow banging of the woman's hand on the ceiling of the cab.

The truck sprayed white dust and gravel as it squealed out onto the highway.

"I told you we would have an adventure," Granny Mueller said.

An old man in a white apron stepped out of The Teepee. He shaded his brow with both hands and looked after the truck.

"God damn Indians," he said.

The little beach and designated swimming area at Spruce Lodge was largely ignored by the lodgers, who very early in the morning would board their rented row boats, each mounted with a small Evinrude outboard, to fish.

Granny Mueller arranged her collapsible lawn chair next to a blanket on the sand for Harris. He would swim circuits around the weathered float until his teeth chattered, then he would warm himself in the sun next to her chair.

"I swam around the float ten times," he told Granny Mueller, clutching himself and shivering in the breeze.

"Ten times! How many times do you think you could swim around that float?"

He considered. He had not been tired, only distracted and a little cold, swimming ten times around. He could, if he kept to his breast stroke, with alternating restful stretches on his back, swim endlessly.

"I could swim around it a hundred times."

"No!"

"A thousand times."

"It would take all night. You'd get dizzy, going round and round. Or you'd *melt*, like Little Black Sambo."

Granny Mueller laughed, but he could not attend to it. *A thousand times.* He could, he probably could, using his breast stroke, which never tired him, and his back stroke.

He went back into the water and slowly breast-stroked a few hundred yards beyond the float. He heard Granny Mueller's voice moving sharply over the water.

"Come *back!* Back, Harris. That's *too far.*"

Harris returned to the shore, submerging and surfacing with each stroke.

"Too far, Harris. You have to stay close to the float."

He looked out across the bay of the lake. The far shore was a stretch of low pines, spiked with the gables of a cottage. Not quite opposite, but most of the way to the far shore and to the right, the wavery shape of another float was visible. He believed he could swim there. He had never witnessed or even imagined such a swim. He wanted to try.

"I want to swim across the lake."

"Across the lake!" Granny Mueller peered out over the water. "How could you do that? What if you got tired and drowned?"

"I will not get tired and drown. Someone could follow me in a boat."

That night in the Lodge after supper, Granny Mueller asked, at Harris's urging, how far it was to the float visible across the bay.

"That would be Norton's float, off to the right?"

"Yes. How far is it?"

"Oh, I don't know. I'd say—three quarters of a mile? A *mile*?"

The Guru heard the pleasing word *mile*. Swimming miles, parts of miles; his swimming would be measured in miles. He felt his heart swell wonderfully. He felt strong.

"We have to do it," he said, "I want to do it, swim across to Norton's Float. We'll do it when daddy gets here. You can follow me, stay close to me, in the boat."

"Harris, what am I going to do with you?" Granny Mueller said, which meant all right. Which meant yes.

The Guru experienced the intervening days as a solemn rite of preparation. Each morning when he and Granny Mueller arrived at the little beach, he walked to the water's edge and fixed his gaze on the distant slab of Norton's Float across the bay. At different hours, in different light, it looked very near at hand, and he could imagine reaching it in minutes, effortlessly; at other moments it looked impossibly, thrillingly far off. In his bed at night the image of the float across shimmering water was fixed in his mind's eye. The image held fast through his sleep and through his dreams as if it were the very center of him.

The day before the scheduled swim, a storm front closed in over Lake Kroehler. He and his father and Granny Mueller played solitaire and checkers as the cabin roof was pelted with downpours. The next morning was cloudless, cool, and very bright. It was agreed that he would begin the swim an hour after lunch, his father and Granny Mueller following close to him in the rowboat assigned to their cabin. After breakfast his father drove out to the bait store and bought a life preserver. Granny Mueller brewed a thermos of hot tea and packed the plastic cooler with sandwiches. A little before one the Guru put on his swimming trunks and walked alone to the beach. He stood ankle deep in the water and watched his Father and Granny Mueller approach, with agonizing slowness, in the rowboat.

The Guru swam out to the float, bellied up onto the deck and said, "Don't get too close to me, or too far away." Then he jumped into the lake, located Norton's float which, from the water line, was only a grey speck against the treeline of the far shore. "There he goes!" he heard Granny Mueller say, and he frog kicked out into the open water.

For quite a while, it occurred to him, he did not think or feel anything. He was aware only of a contraction and extension of his legs and arms as he dipped and surfaced. His breaststroke never seemed to tire him, although when he went slowly, he felt himself dropping too far below the surface between breaths. He did not want to go too slowly, or too fast. Less because he was tired than because he was curious, he turned over on his back. The lodge float was disappointingly near beyond his toes. Turning over, he spotted Norton's float, again a distant speck. There was no noticeable progress. He experienced something like an all-body complaint. *I will swim,* he told himself, *until I cannot move.*

As he made his way out of the protected inlet of the resort, he felt a steady breeze at his ears as he came up for breath, and the surface of the water was now ruffled by irregular little waves. If he did not thrust his chin effortfully out and up when he surfaced, the waves would splash into his mouth, choking and stalling him. Realizing that it was discouraging to keep siting the distant and unchanging float out ahead, he resolved to clear his mind of all thought and swim.

"Harris!" his father's voice was calling out. "Harris!" It was his father and Granny Mueller both. *"Harris!"* He stopped, dog-paddling in place, blinking the water from his eyes.

"Harris," his father was shouting from the boat, "I think you're going the wrong way, old man. You're going kind of *sideways.* The float's *this* way, to the *left.*" His father was gesturing over his shoulder.

He was confused. It made him tired to be dog paddling. He was angry at being tired, at having to talk. Then he realized that his father and Granny Mueller were laughing.

"Not funny," he said, but the clenched coldness along his jaw made it hard for him to talk, and they could not hear. *They cannot hear,* he realized angrily, *because they are too far away.*

"Closer!" he tried to say, but it sounded in his own ears like *cloder.* Without seeming to hurry, his father maneuvered the boat to within a few feet of his head. The waves plopped and slapped against the hull.

"Stay closer," he told them. "Go ahead of me, so I can see where to go."

"Had enough?" Granny Mueller asked.

"No!" the Guru gestured ahead with one hand, "Go, but stay close."

"You let us know when you've had enough."

The Guru made a sharp image of himself sitting on the bow of the rowboat, swaddled with dry towels and eating Granny Mueller's sandwiches. He imagined sitting perfectly still, feeling light as air, the sun pressing pleasingly on his dry face. Then he knew: *temptations.* He frog kicked out after the stern of the rowboat.

The Guru let his mind wander as he swam, and he felt much better. He pictured reaching Norton's float, stepping exhausted and happy up the ladder to the deck. He thought about being rowed over the sunny lake back to the resort. He thought about dinner that night in the lodge. He thought about his new-smelling blue jeans from Sears and his red plaid flannel shirt. At the lodge he would order a hamburger with catsup. He would order extra french fries. He would have Pepsis. He dipped and surfaced, gulping then expelling the air. Sometimes the wind picked up and met his face, and he felt that he was almost standing upright in the water, rather than lying out over the surface. He saw his father rest the oars on the gunwales between strokes. Every few minutes Granny Mueller would lean over the stern and say, "How are you doing? Tell us when you've had enough" or, occasionally, "You're doing great."

It tired him to try to answer, so he continued swimming, dropping, stroking, kicking, surfacing for air. He was aware of some muffled talk in the boat, but he could not make out what was being said. Then he surfaced and Granny Mueller exclaimed clearly, "You're half-way there, Harris! Half-way home."

Half-way. *Home*. He turned over on his back and, by craning his neck, saw that it was true. The float back at the lodge was now the same distant mass as Norton's Float out ahead of them.

The Guru's strokes grew shorter and his breaths more frequent. His exhalations now sounded loudly in his ears. He knew now that he needed longer stretches on his back, even though he felt it was a slower stroke. But on his back he could breathe continuously, except when a wave broke over his brow onto his face and choked him.

Turning back over on his stomach, he caught a glimpse of his father and grandmother which unsettled him. His father was idling at the oars. His face and Granny Mueller's face had grown slack. *They were bored.*

Suddenly, powerfully, he felt as if he was going to cry. *Until I cannot move*, he told himself and frog kicked ahead with a sickening exertion.

He had been on his back for a long time and was starting to feel sleepy. He found it hard to keep thinking about Norton's Float. He could imagine forgetting about it altogether.

"Almost there, Harris," Granny Mueller was saying. "Just a few hundred more yards."

His father's voice: "You've got it licked, old man."

He turned over. He did not want to reach the float paddling weakly on his back. He stroked and kicked in the direction of the float. He could see it now, first on one side then on the other side of the rowboat's stern, and it now looked imposing on its hollow black drums. The distance ahead was deceptive; the float was both near and defiantly far. The interval refused to close. He felt it again——*temptation,* a desire to loop an arm over the stern of the rowboat and rest.

He turned over on his back, taking close, quick breaths.

"You all right, old man?"

It would be all right he knew now, to arrive on his back. It would be all right even to sleep on the water. Protected by the wooded arm of another cove, the lake had become smooth again. If he could sleep, if he could sleep without his head dropping under the honey-colored water—

"Don't bump your *head,*" Granny Mueller was saying. He turned over to look and there, a yard in front of him, was the grey painted ladder of Norton's Float.

He clasped the sides of the ladder and pulled his legs up the rungs. He felt leaden, leaden with water. Then he was standing, chilly and shivering, on the deck of the float.

"Ta-*dah!*" Granny Mueller sang out. "The champion. You *did it*, Harris. You are my champion."

His arms and legs trembled and his teeth chattered as he eased himself into the bow seat of the rowboat. He let Granny Mueller drape his shoulders and legs with beach towels radiant with the heat of the afternoon sun. Now his father was rowing steadily, leaning into his strokes, and Granny Mueller was rustling through wax paper in the cooler.

He felt it begin warmly below his heart, a release of great certainty and pleasure. It moved in waves, in sweet vibrations all through him, thrilling the underside of his chin, the base of his skull, each gladness surpassed by the surge of the next. It was so exquisitely finished, so hard, so impossible yet now *accomplished*.

The Guru could hear the *slip-slop* of the water against the bow behind him as he watched Norton's Float recede over the lake.

He let the towel slip from his dry shoulders. He let the Illusion of Effort dissolve in the bright air.

7

Granny Mueller and the Bears

Esther, the cheerful blond woman who tended the desk at the lodge, asked Harris and Granny Mueller if they had been to the dump to see the bears.

Bears! The Guru felt tingling at the back of his neck as Granny Mueller made inquiries.

"What *kind* of bears?" he asked suddenly.

They were brown bears, and they liked to visit the dump on Saturdays, after the resorts made their garbage runs. The hour or two after it got dark, Esther said, was the best time to see them.

"But stay in your car!" She said with wide eyes, and then she laughed.

There was a partial set of the *Encyclopedia Americana* in the lodge sitting room. He and Granny Mueller picked out Volume II, Baal-Byzantium, and sat down together to read the entry on Bears. Brown bears, Granny Mueller read aloud, were related to the great Grizzlies of the Northwest. They were bigger and more dangerous to man than the smaller, more evasive black bears indigenous to the eastern states.

So there were brown bears, he thought excitedly, just a few miles down the road from the lodge with its cheerful circle of closely mown grass, its flapping flag on the flag pole, shuffle board courts, docks of creaking, clanking boats. He could picture brown bears moving among the scrubby pines beyond the cluster of cottages. With the revelation of the bears the resort—no, the whole world—felt more thrillingly charged, more dangerous.

That Saturday Granny Mueller promised to take him to the drive-in in Little Falls, and now, to his giddy pleasure, they would stop in at the dump on the way back. They would look for bears in the dark from the safe front seat of the locked Ford. This would be nothing like the zoo. He wondered whether the experience he was both craving and dreading was possible in the world outside of dreams.

The movie was *Song of the South*, and except to note its unreal sweetness—he kept images of a retreating blue-bird and the purply-brown pelts of the animated creatures—he was too excited to concentrate. Granny Mueller had been on edge and crabby because the teenage boys in the neighboring cars were loud and unpleasant, calling out to one another from their open window, using swear words.

"They're drinking. They're all drinking," Granny Mueller said, and she left him by himself while she went off to find someone in charge. He sat very still in the passenger seat. He wanted to be invisible. Outside Granny Mueller's window, louder than the voices coming from the speaker fitted into the window, he heard:

"Where the hell is Pete?"

"I don't know, probably shit-faced."

Granny Mueller returned to the car and said nothing. Her face was set angrily. He was aware that someone had come and was walking between the cars shining a flashlight. A man was telling the boys in the car next to them to go.

The air was unbreathable. The Guru felt a pressure like a board pressed hard against his belly and chest.

The car next to him screamed and squealed in reverse. The engine roared.

"And are we going to get our fucking *money* back?"

Car horns from seemingly all over were honking in complaint. He did not want to turn his head.

They left *Song of the South* early. Granny Mueller did not explain. She replaced the window speaker on its stand and started the engine.

They drove in silence, and he now felt a sour foreboding about the dump.

Hand made signs directed them from the two-lane macadam road to a sandy lane which opened onto a clearing of packed earth. Directly ahead was a crescent shaped mound, eight or ten feet high, of bull-dozed refuse. The crescent spanned a few hundred yards, and every few feet there were wisps of smoke from smoldering fires. The sour tang of burning garbage made the corners of his eyes sting.

Bags and cans and tissues were illuminated garishly by the headlights of what they now saw were dozens of cars and trucks parked haphazardly before the crescent. There was trouble, an aggravating tension in the air, exactly as it had been at the drive-in. Granny Mueller brought the Ford to a stop but did not turn off the motor.

"I don't know," she said without looking at him.

The voices and revving engines beyond the Ford's windows sounded like the drive-in. He could hear, but did not want to differentiate, hooting, cursing, eruptions of laughter that sounded like barking. A shirtless man descended from the cab of his truck, gyrated suggestively for a minute in the glare of the headlights, then turned and threw the beer bottles he held in each hand onto the mound of rubbish.

"Hey, bears," he shouted into the darkness beyond the rubble. "You like Hamm's? You drink Hamm's?"

He returned to his truck but did not get back into the cab. He could not open the door.

"O.K., very funny, now open up." There was more pulling on the door handle, then he pounded on the door, the window.

"Open the fucking door, you hear me? *Open it*, shithead."

From down the crescent, the Guru heard: "There's one, over there!" Then laughter.

"*Open it!*"

"I think we've had enough of this," Granny Mueller said, and she backed up, turned the wheel sharply, and steered down the sandy path to the road. Just before the turn off to the lodge, she brought the Ford to a gradual stop and whispered, "What's that?"

A low-slung smoky presence on the shoulder of the road crouched in the beam of the headlights. The size of a small dog, it had a sharp aggressive snout, like a rat's, but more flattened at the tip. Its fur was dirty white, and it looked wet, oily. Directly in front of the car, it turned its head defiantly into the headlights, and its eyes glowed with a pinkish green iridescence.

"That's a possum," Granny Mueller said.

The Guru thought it was pure malevolence, sheer animal ugliness.

The following Saturday morning as they packed up to leave Spruce Lodge, he was overcome by Granny Mueller's sweetness to him and by the enormity of love he felt for her. His father had gone ahead to Chicago after breakfast, and there was a profound, slightly sad peace in the cabin.

"Have I got all your dirty things?" She asked, standing in the doorway to his room. "Your socks?"

He had taken care to make his bed, to pull the sheets and blankets tight, so no wrinkle showed, even though it was the last day and the staff would pull up the bedding and take it off to the laundry. He had wanted to leave that clean sign of himself. He was about to close his suitcase when Granny Mueller appeared.

"May I check the packing job?" she asked.

"Yes." He had folded and stacked his clothes neatly, tying them loosely in place with the shiny cloth straps.

"A-plus, Harris," she said, then she bent low and drew him into her cushiony warmth. She lightly kissed his neck, his ears, the side of his head. It made his skin tingle, and he shuddered.

"I don't think I have ever had a better traveling companion," she said, tightening her embrace for emphasis before releasing him.

He knew.

As they pulled away from the lodge, Granny Mueller was smiling as if she was about to tell him a joke or a secret. He waited, but she only hummed the tune, "How Much is that Doggy in the Window."

"It will be dark when we get home," he said.

"It will be very dark."

Granny Mueller slowed the car, and turned down a narrow sandy lane.

"I thought we would make a last stop at the dump," she said, smiling but not looking at him.

The sky overhead was darkly overcast, and there were no other cars, only the crescent of pungent rubble, wispy traces of smoke. Granny Mueller switched off the motor. It felt nice for him to be there in the quiet by themselves. A few drops of rain spattered loudly on the windshield.

"I wonder if bears like the daylight?" she asked.

They talked, warmly, remembering the special moments of their stay. They talked about the Great Swim. Granny Mueller said, "Who would have imagined," and he smiled, knowing that he had. He had imagined it, perfectly.

The Guru was very happy sitting in the Ford, talking about the Swim and the best meals and the solitaire "Championship." The rain drops plopping noisily on the roof of the car helped to enclose them under the blue-black sky.

"Well," Granny Mueller said at length, "looking at her watch, "I guess bears *don't* like daytime."

She started the car, looked over her shoulder to back up, then turned off the ignition.

"*Harris!*" she whispered hoarsely. "Look out the back window."

At first he did not see them, and then there they were, three brownish yellow bears, their broad backs hunched behind their powerful shoulders as they made their way over the crest of the rubble at the far end of the crescent. For a minute or two they foraged around the base of the mound, and he wished the oval of the rear window were less streaky with rain. Then, apparently aware of the car, one of them stood up on its hind legs and looked their way.

The Guru turned around and knelt up against the seat back in order to see better.

"He's coming to see us," said Granny Mueller softly, as the bear approached the Ford.

"Are the doors locked?" he asked, now on edge.

"It's all right," Granny Mueller said, "Bears don't know how to open car doors." The bear had reared up on its hind legs again and was standing directly behind the trunk. The coarse fur of its breast completely filled the back window. "But," she said, "You may push the buttons down if you like.

Together they scrambled to lock all four car doors.

Perhaps stimulated by the movement inside, the bear moved around to the passenger side of the car. The Guru edged in closer to Granny Mueller. He glanced out at the bear without turning. It had the head of a great, unfeeling dog.

"It's all right, Harris," Granny Mueller said softly, "He doesn't want to harm us. He is just curious."

"Is the bear as big as the car?" he asked.

"I think," Granny Mueller said, considering, "he is as big as half of the car."

The bear extended itself and they could hear its paws come to rest heavily on the roof. The Guru could feel the car incline slightly to his side.

The Guru drew in his breath sharply.

"Have we seen enough of the bear?" Granny Mueller asked, closing her fingers over the keys in the ignition.

"I don't know," he said.

The bear stepped back a little from the side of the car, bracing himself with a paw against the passenger seat window. Now the Guru turned to look and saw the pads of the bear's paw were purple and cracked, like worn leather. Without thinking, he placed his palm on the glass opposite the paw.

"That's nice," Granny Mueller said.

"Yes."

"Are you saying good-bye and thank you?"

"Yes."

Granny Mueller started the motor, and the bear drew away from the car and bounded back to the others. All three watched attentively as Granny Mueller reversed the car and drove, very slowly, out of the enclosure toward the road.

"You do well with bears," Granny Mueller said. "You are a big boy today, Harris."

Yes.

8

The Unity of All Life

The third and last summer Granny Mueller took him to Lake Kroehler, the Guru experienced the Unity of All Life.

On Friday morning, a day before their departure back to Palatine, the Guru stood at the end of the cabin dock, his back to the water, surveying the sun-blanched compound. He marveled again at what he was beginning to call the Time Cages, the partial and restricted understanding of things due simply to the rest of it being not yet revealed.

He was thinking, specifically, of Spruce Lodge Resort itself and Lake Kroehler. Three summers earlier, when he was ten, it had consisted of their cabin, the lodge, the pleasure of the hamburgers, the worn path to the beach, the water, the Great Swim and then, finally, the bears at the dump. He had pictured, after Esther revealed their existence, brown bears lumbering and snorting in the pinewoods beyond the circle of cabins. He had not known, or been shown, that the resort was far more complex, the surrounding woods still more complex. There were, he knew now, trails. The trails, some of them, went for miles, led to and over streambeds which cut deep ravines into limestone, creating mossy canyons. The streams themselves opened into other bays of the lake. The long trail to Barrett's Lane led over a series of shallow, pebbly streams to the Little Dunes above the marshes of Kroehler Flowage. All of this, and of course vastly more, was there, was true, when he was ten, but it had been inaccessible from that Time Cage.

Shedding that Time Cage, he knew, was an invitation to shed every Time Cage—including this Moment of Present Vision. The Guru laughed out loud. Though scanning the roofline of their cabin, he could see in his mind's eye the flashing facets of the lake behind him. *Because it is there.* The Guru raised another shout of laughter.

Yesterday had been overcast with periodic showers, but the day before he and Granny Mueller had hiked Barrett's Lane until they reached the first stream. There Granny Mueller had wanted to turn back so that she could rest before dinner. Today, he determined, he would shed the Time Cage, go further, perhaps to the end of the dunes. The idea of scaling and descending the hillocks of warm sand excited him. He saw himself trudging through the dunes, naked and brown, carrying his clothes in a bunched ball under his arm. In the hot dunes he would feel he was the First Man. A breeze from the water played over his arms and the backs of his legs. The pleasure of it made him rise up on his toes and stretch himself.

"Are you sure," Granny Mueller said slowly, when he announced his intended hike. "Be sure to wind your watch," she told him and then got up to pack his lunch.

The Guru went to his bureau, removed the bone-handled hunting knife in its stiff leather sheath from the top drawer, pressed it down under his belt to the hilt. For an instant the Guru imagined not returning, sleeping in the dunes under the stars, the next day moving on. *It would require money.*

The Guru felt charged with energy and full of anticipation as he set off along the path behind the lodge. Rust colored pine needles covered the double ruts of the trail, and his sneakers felt buoyant and cushioned as he made his way. His grip closed tightly over the rolled top of his lunch bag, and he made a little hum of pleasure at the thought of sitting in shaded solitude, or perhaps at the edge of the sunny dunes, eating his lunch. *Alone, the First Man.*

In less than an hour he reached the log bridge to Barrett Lane. With Granny Mueller, it had taken twice that long. It was too early for lunch, but there was a refuse barrel by the bridge rail, and he could throw away the remains of his lunch and the Pepsi bottle if he ate there. The rush of the little brook over the stones cleared the Guru's head of thought, and he was barely aware of the slightly sour mush of liverwurst and relish against his palate. The Pepsi retained some of its chill from the refrigerator, and the carbonation made a familiar burn at the back of his nostrils. But as he wadded the bag around the empty bottle and dropped it into the bin, he could not specifically remember having eaten.

The distractedness hung about his head like a mist as he proceeded along Barrett Lane. The pines and birches and tangles of ferns on either side seemed invariable, and he was unsure whether he had been walking a short or long time. He resisted looking at his watch; the idea of knowing the precise time made him feel anxious, hopeless. His gaze fixed a few feet ahead on the path, he gripped the bone handle of his hunting knife with his right hand. He wanted to close his eyes, to walk on without seeing. He wanted to walk on without walking.

At length the trees and scrub became more scattered and spare, and the earth of the path gave way to sand. Now there was a bright horizon, and the powerful light made the Guru feel wide-awake. The sandy indentation of the path flattened out and disappeared. A few feet ahead the sand wavered and shimmered under a glassy sheet of water where three or four rivulets converged from out of the woods behind. This was where Granny Mueller had wanted to turn back.

The ripply flow of water passed over the thick rubber soles of his sneakers, and he felt the cold under the arches of his feet as he stepped across. The rounded pebbles before him gleamed like glass beneath the sparkling water. On the far side his shoes and socks squelched and plopped with each step, so he undid his sneakers, stuffed the soggy socks up into the toes, tied the laces together and proceeded into the dunes. The sneakers, banging gently over his shoulder as he walked, seemed to be speaking to him in a reassuring way.

When he passed through the first crease in the dunes, he could no longer, when he turned back to look, see the woods behind. The experience of only great heaves of sand on all sides was an overwhelming pleasure, a liberating release. Each step was now effortful, after a while making his calves and the arches of his feet ache, but when he stopped to rest, the stored radiance of the sand rose up through his soles, and he was happy.

It occurred to the Guru that he had lost track of the direction he was moving. Trudging up to the crest of the highest dune before him, he looked out over the serration of dune tops and saw the sun flashing whitely on the waves of the lake. Behind him he could see the green treetops of the woods. Side-stepping and sliding down to the base of the dune, he knew that he was held, concealed perfectly.

The Guru undressed. He rolled his shorts and tee shirt together and lay the roll on top of his sneakers. The gusts off the open lake would have been chilly without the bright sun overhead. The Guru felt the sun's dry force on his shoulders, belly, and legs, then the caress of a breeze. Taking care not to lose sight of the mound of his clothes, he walked naked through the sculpted hollows. Around him was only sand, rosy in the shadows, khaki, wheat, and shimmering white where sunlight met the crests. *A world of this*, he thought. *Another world.* A breeze played over his face, his knees, the tip of his penis. He extended his arms wide and gave himself up to an almost unbearable surge of pleasure. The pleasure receded, then rose up again and held him in its current. The Guru released a sob. *Laughing and crying.*

He made his way to his clothes. Feeling suddenly very tired, he lay out on the warm sand, pillowing his head on the roll. A fly alighted on his shoulder, and a gust carried it off. The Guru spread his legs, opened his arms to the sun. *This has always been true.* Sleepily, he embraced the impossibility of living in the dunes, of never leaving.

The Guru awoke with a chill. The sun had progressed beyond the crest of the dunes before his feet, and a grey, finished light played on the sand.

He sat up and dressed. His sneakers and socks were still wet, so he slung them over his shoulder until he reached the first sandy fingers of the stream bed. He cast a long, distinct shadow over the rippling water, insistently gurgling as it passed over the stones.

Midstream, the Guru bent over to inspect the glassy bottom, and as he stared, the pebbles began to move. But they were not pebbles; they were the tiny spines of needle-thin minnows hovering and darting among the mossy rocks. Then the rocks themselves seemed to move. But they were not rocks; they were crayfish, and at a movement of his soaked sneaker, they would rouse themselves from the texture of the stream bottom, scuttle on tarnished claws over the pebbles, let the current carry them, then fold again into their stillness. The Guru stepped up the stream toward the woods until it deepened. The water darkened to the color of honey, of Pepsi. Then, without seeming to have arrived, three little iridescent fish were nosing to within an inch of his ankles. *It is all connected*, he realized, *all alive.*

Stepping out of the stream, the Guru scanned the treeline until he located the opening to Barrett Lane. The path into the woods looked tunneled, dark, and it occurred to him to look at his watch: *six.*

He squeezed a few drops of water from his socks. Then dropped to one knee to put on his sneakers. Looking up—*a signal*—he stilled his hands as a deer, its flank lit coppery red by the declining sun, stepped noiselessly from the woods. The deer paused, cocked its head in his direction, then proceeded to the edge of the stream. As the Guru stood up, another deer, then another, then another emerged from the darkening green. He turned, and on his other side too, deer had moved to the water to drink. *As they always have.* The Guru mouthed the words silently. He was the First Man.

He looked at his watch again. *After six.* Barrett Lane grew darker as sand gave way to earth and pine needles. *I will have to run.* Running, his feet plopping and slopping in his wet shoes, he knew he would not have to see them. There would just be the blur of passing woods.

9
Rapture in the Bath

Forrester slid back the glass panel and turned in his seat to address the Guru.

"If you're going to sit here for a while, I think I'll get out and stretch my legs. Maybe take a little walk."

The Guru was slow to rise up out of his reverie. He met Forrester's questioning gaze and said nothing.

"Maybe take a walk around the block," Forrester repeated.

"You want to get out. And walk." The Guru spoke very deliberately.

"Yes. I could use a little air. Stretch my legs."

"I suppose it is time to see my father."

Forrester was confused, then he remembered: Schaumberg, the Assisted Living Center.

"So you're ready to go on to Schaumberg? Probably a good idea if you want to be back to the Sheraton for dinner."

"Yes." Said the Guru, "We should move on."

As the Guru felt the engine start, he experienced a wrenching spasm of sadness. He fixed the little grey house in his gaze, closed his eyes. This would be the last of Palatine.

The Town Car moved forward, paused at the stop sign, then turned down Walnut away from the grey house. The Guru felt drawn back, drawn back into the house, down past the kitchen along the hallway to the back bathroom. He had forgotten about the bath.

He had loved to take baths. Granny Mueller would fill the tub with water that was bearably, but not stingingly, not. He liked to lie back, submerged up to his chin. The water would rise to within a few inches of the rim of the tub. He made slippery lather with the soap, learned to hold and release the suds in his cupped hands. He would roll about in the grey soapy water until it grew tepid. In the bath, his sphere of action and imagination contracted to the dimension of the tub. Granny Mueller never disturbed him, and he would close his eyes, the comforting cover of water warming him everywhere, warming even his throat and the soft skin under his chin. In the bath he was free to return. He could close his eyes tight, contort his face, make low humming songs, voice his secret words, incanting the phrases over and over.

In the bath one chilly Saturday evening the Guru experienced Body Rapture. It was the autumn after the final trip to Lake Kroehler and he was revisiting the days in his mind's eye. Again and again he recalled the Unity: the kaleidoscopic movement of minnows and crayfish on the stream floor, the silent emergence of the deer. Then he was back in the dunes, entering the dunes. The charged aloneness and the beautiful, beckoning contours of sand aroused the ache of his longing. Again he was undressing, rolling up his shorts and tee shirt, and then he was walking, naked in the heat, naked in the caressing breeze. He let the current overwhelm him, and all the while he had been stroking himself, and his penis was now hard and white, like a bone, and there was a mounting discomfort as, rhythmically, he slapped it down into the bath water. Behind his eyes, he was standing, arms extended, naked in the breeze of the dunes. He lay back in the tub, the warm water closing in over his ears. His slapping quickened, and the feeling rushed from the base of his skull, down along his spine, and erupted in a delicious, almost sickening succession of pleasures as the dunes became the bath, and the bath became the Golden World.

The Guru sat up in the tub. His heart and belly felt depleted, weak. His penis, still hard, tingled unpleasantly at his touch. But it had happened. He had been held fast in its throbbing. *It had happened*, the Guru realized. *I can go there.*

10
Diet of Worms

Forrester stopped at the sign opposite Grace Lutheran Church, and as he accelerated through the intersection, he looked into the rear view mirror and saw that the Guru was staring straight ahead. He looked startled, angry.

The Guru recognized the familiar stone steps up to the varnished wooden doors of the church. He felt the deadening weight and turned away.

In the sadness of Junior High School, some time before the Resolution to Perfection, Granny Mueller had determined to take him to church. He remembered hearing her discussing it with his father in the kitchen while he was in the living room watching TV. "You should take him." Granny Mueller said, "it would do you good." His father was not sure. "He should at least be *exposed*."

It did not surprise him that one Sunday morning in the fall of his sixth grade year, it was not his father but Granny Mueller who, wearing a shiny brown dress and a hat affixed to her hair with

a long pin, escorted him along the sidewalks of Palatine to Grace
Lutheran Church.

Seated in their pew before the service began, the Guru was
aware of an oppressive heaviness. The hushed voices of the other
early arrivals hung in the air. There was the harsh echo of an occasional cough. Grey stone walls and columns rose to a high vaulted
ceiling of dark wood. The leaded grids of the stained glass windows seemed to imprison the biblical figures and animals cartooned
in glowing facets. The church, he thought, squinting up into the
mosaic of blue and green and red glass, was like a giant jewelry box,
and he was inside.

A tentative treble line of organ music entered the vaulted
atmosphere. It sounded to the Guru nasal and sinister. It sounded
as if it were sneaking into the sanctuary. Then all at once there
were the deep flatulent chords of the full organ. The Guru looked
up into Granny Mueller's eyes. "This is terrible."

Without thinking they rose with the congregation to sing.
The other worshippers had extracted hymnals from the wooden
racks built into the pew backs and had located the hymn. Granny
Mueller, arriving before the greeters, had not received an Order
of Service. She took a hymnal from the rack and craned to see a
page number in her seatmate's open book. At length she gave up,
closed the hymnal in her hands, and hummed an approximation of
the hymn deep in her throat. The Guru thought the song sounded

unpleasantly insistent. He pictured a crowd of angry people from long ago marching out the gate of a walled city.

The prayers and responses and announcements seemed to hover unreally just below the timbered ceiling. The words were articulated clearly enough, but the Guru could not make sense of them. Several times he heard: *in the name of the father. In* the name— he could not see it.

It was the same, he decided, with the hymns. The congregation sang out, but as he listened the voices somehow combined with the organ to make the words unintelligible. As they sang the Guru looked around. A little awkwardly, he turned to look at the people behind him, then up at those standing in the balcony. *They don't like it. Nobody wants this.*

The congregation was seated, there was a little volley of throat-clearing and coughing, and then the sermon began.

The Guru sat up attentively. The pastor wore a black robe. His hair was a crew cut, quite long, a table top of bristly hair. The lights over the pulpit flashed in the lenses of his glasses which made his expressions and gestures look effortful and blind. The pastor spoke forcefully, suddenly emphasizing words and phrases in a way that made the Guru's diaphragm contract.

The sermon was about refereeing a church league basketball game, and immediately the Guru was drawn into it. He felt an almost unbearable fascination imagining the stocky figure of the pastor, with his high brush cut hair, his startling inflections, moving about a gymnasium full of boys. The Guru pictured the boys in his school. *They would not like him*, he mused. *They would not pay attention.*

The pastor was telling about a boy who had fouled other players repeatedly and intentionally. The pastor said he called the fouls. *Called them.* The boy lost his temper, and the pastor told how he drew him apart from the other players, because he knew the boy was upset. He had taken care to speak softly and kindly to the boy. The pastor had said—he repeated it in a slow dramatic whisper— "You don't really want to play that way, do you, son?" The pastor paused. He gripped the sides of the pulpit with his hands and leaned forward. "And do you know what he did? Do you know what the young man said to me?" Another pause. The pastor stood up straight. "He cursed me. The boy cursed me."

The pastor went on, but the Guru wanted to know what the boy had said. *Cursed him. What was the curse?* Now the pastor was telling a story about Jesus from the bible. The Guru was distracted and barely listened. He wanted to know about the boy who cursed. He wondered if the boy went to the Junior High, wondered excitedly if they would meet.

He could not quite reenter the sermon. Several times before closing the pastor repeated the phrase "pearls before swine." The

Guru mouthed "swine" and looked questioningly up at Granny Mueller. "Pigs," she whispered. *Pearls before pigs.* The Guru imagined round milky pearls rolling about the feet of pigs. He knew the pigs wouldn't want them, wouldn't want pearls.

It had been prearranged that he would return to Grace Lutheran Church that afternoon to attend Communicants Class. Granny Mueller explained that this would be like a school. It would be like a school on Sunday afternoon, and in a few weeks he would be ready to be confirmed as a member of the church.

"What if I am not a member?" He asked Granny Mueller as they walked back to West Walnut Street.

"You should try it," She said.

After lunch Granny Mueller surprised him by giving him a bible. It was bound in deep red leather, and there was smooth marbled paper inside the front and back covers. The pages were delicately, transparently thin, and when he closed the book, he saw that their edges were tinted gold. The bible felt ancient, exquisite in his hands. "Look," Granny Mueller said, tapping the lower right hand corner of the cover. *H.M.* was imprinted in gold leaf.

The Guru held tightly to his new bible as he returned to Grace Lutheran Church for Communicants Class. He entered the narthex and peered inside. There was nobody in the sanctuary. He wandered hesitantly through unlocked doors from hallway to hallway until he heard voices.

In contrast to the silent passages of the church, the Sunday school room where the communicants met was noisy and anarchic. When he entered, about twenty children, five or six of the faces familiar to him from Junior High, were seated around low tables. One of the teachers, a slender man wearing a white shirt that showed his undershirt beneath, greeted him and asked his name.

"So you're new to us this week. Class—*people*, this is Harris Mueller, and he'll be joining the class."

There were no more places at the low nursery tables, so the Guru drew a chair up behind Andy Jacobson, a boy he knew. Andy Jacobson was tall and bony. His rust-colored hair grew back from his forehead in crinkly waves. He turned back to the Guru, shielding his mouth with one hand and said, "this really stinks."

The Communicants Class had begun three weeks earlier, and the teachers were checking the progress of the candidates' preparation at home that week. As the adults bent over to confer with each candidate, the other children dissolved into noisy chatter.

"Class, *people*," the man in the white shirt said periodically. The Guru felt his stomach tighten. He looked at his watch. Only a few minutes had passed.

They were quizzed on the books of the Old Testament, which they had been assigned to memorize in order. The Guru was excused from reciting because he was new. Only a few of the girls had prepared. A blond boy with a red face was mimicking the girls. "*Gen*esis, *Exo*dus, Lev*it*icus. Doo—that's all I know." Directly in front of the Guru Andy Jacobson poked the point of his pencil into the frizzy braids of a girl named Monica he recognized from the Junior High. Absently she batted a hand at the annoyance without turning around. Andy Jacobson turned conspiratorially to the Guru, his eyes widened crazily, then returned his attention to Monica, reinserting his pencil into her braids. She twisted around and said sharply, "You cut that out!"

Andy Jacobson dropped his arm to his side, concealing the pencil.

"What? What did I do?"

"Stupid *idiot.*"

"Class, *People*—"

"Genesis, Exodus, Deuteronomy—that's all I know."

Over the mounting chatter the teachers exhorted the communicants to do better, to come prepared next week. After the man in the white shirt said this, he turned to the other teacher, a woman in a wrinkled, confining-looking black skirt and a red shiny blouse, and said, "Mrs. Foster, would you like to add anything?" Mrs. Foster repeated the same things the man in the white shirt had said.

The Guru looked again at his watch. Seemingly no time had passed.

Next the teachers asked the class questions about the chapter they were assigned to read from a brightly colored book called *Life of Luther*. The Guru had not been given the book, so he was asked to look on with Andy Jacobson. No one knew, or was willing to say, what was an Indulgence, what Martin Luther saw on his pilgrimage to Rome, what salvation by grace meant, what the Ninety-Five Theses were.

The teachers decided that they would read the chapter aloud together. Each communicant read several paragraphs haltingly, without inflection. "And *now* can you see," Mrs. Foster interrupted Monica's reading, "Why Martin Luther would object to paying an Indulgence?" No one spoke.

Andy Jacobson read next. He stumbled or stopped altogether when he reached unfamiliar words, the names of German people or cities. When the teacher enunciated the word, Andy Jacobson said "O.K." and giggled nervously.

Next was the Guru's turn. He did not want to read, but he recited the specified lines clearly and quickly. No thought entered his head as he read. Then—he heard the words sounding in his ears as if spoken by somebody else—the class erupted in laughter when he said "Diet of Worms."

For a while the class could not be quieted.

"A diet is a *meeting*," Mrs. Foster was saying over the din. "Worms is a *city*."

The Guru felt his own disgust mounting as he pictured a moist tangle of red worms, worms on a plate.

"Class, *people*. This is not funny."

Over supper Granny Mueller said. "It can't have been as bad as all that? What was so bad about it."

He knew he could not explain. He could not explain the gaping awfulness of Andy Jacobson's face as he bothered Monica's braids or when he stumbled trying to read aloud. Again he pictured the tangle of worms on a plate. *Diet of Worms*.

"It wasn't right," he said.

"I think you should give it another try."

"No, I can't. Please," he said, looking hard in Granny Mueller's eyes. "I can't. But I will read the bible."

11
The Tie Rack

Forrester identified himself to the uniformed attendant at the gated entrance to Villa Serena. Approved, he nosed the Town Car slowly along the curved lanes, following the arrowed signs to the Assisted Living Center.

"Here we are," Forrester said through the open panel. "I'll drop you here in front and park over in the lot. When you come out, I'll pull up."

"Very good," said the Guru, planting a heavy leg on the pavement. He felt a stab of pain deep in his abdomen, then the familiar dull ache as he stood up to walk. As Forrester advanced, he could see the Guru's deep red robe in the side view mirror. The Guru extended his arms wide on each side and rotated his torso slowly. *Huge*, Forrester said to himself. *Strange, strange guy.*

The reception area of the Assisted Living Center was clean and bright and smelled of antiseptic and fresh flowers. A pleasant faced black woman regarded the Guru with smiling curiosity as he approached the desk.

"I am here to see Otto Mueller. My father."

"Yes, welcome." Her face clouded. "So you are Mr. Mueller's *son?*" She smiled at the Guru with a benign incredulity.

"His one and only."

"Let me go see if I can find him. I'll be right back."

The Guru seated himself on a vinyl covered chair opposite the desk. Filtered strings were playing not quite audibly through a speaker overhead. A frail woman bent over an aluminum walker made her way past him. She did not turn to look.

The Guru recalled his father as a young man in his dark green golf shirt. He saw the skin drawn tightly along his jaw, revealing the bony lower orbits of his dark eyes. He remembered his father coming to take him home from the school nurse's office, saw the reticent, hurt look on his face. His father had not known what to say.

He was aware that the receptionist had returned only when she began to speak.

"Mr. Mueller?"

The Guru looked up into her eyes, confused. "Sir," she said patiently, "Your father is in his room. I can take you to him."

The Guru did not glance inside any of the open doorways to the residents' suites as they walked together along the immaculate hallway. The receptionist said, "I told him you were here, that he had a visitor. I said 'your son has come to see you.' He is a little confused, you know, and I wasn't able to tell him your name. I told him that you were—his son was—here and that I would bring you to him."

"And what did he say?" The Guru asked.

"He said 'California.'"

"Ah, yes."

When they entered his father's suite, he was sitting up fully clothed on his bed. In contrast to the muted fluorescence of the corridor, the room was brilliant with afternoon sunlight. The Guru noted his father's crisp green shirt, still showing its laundered creases. His khaki trousers too were starched and sharply creased. They were belted high up on his rib cage, creating an impression that his father was overwhelmed, shrinking into his clothes. On his feet were athletic shoes of a complex design, quite new.

"Mr. Mueller," the receptionist said, "I've brought your son here to see you. He's come to see you."

The Guru's father looked hopefully up at the figure of his son. He seemed about to speak but then hesitated.

"I don't know," he said, a trace of fear in his pale eyes, "I don't know why nobody told me."

"But I did tell you, Mr. Mueller," the receptionist said brightly. "I did tell you. And now here he is, for a visit." She looked up sharply at the Guru. "I'll leave you now so you can talk. Dinner is at 5:45. You are welcome to stay for dinner. Would you like me to fill out a resident's guest card?"

"No, thank you."

The Guru seated himself on a chair on the window side of the room, but aware that the sun was in his father's eyes, he carried the chair around to the other side of the bed. His father followed his movements with a troubled look.

"What are you doing?" he said.

"Moving over here where the light won't hurt your eyes." The Guru seated himself and looked deeply into his father's eyes. His father appeared clean, frail, delicate in his bones. "Are you feeling well?"

"Yes, I am."

"That's good. Is this a good place to be?"

"Yes, it is."

"Do you have friends here?"

His father hesitated. "Are you here for the contest?"

"The contest? What contest would that be?"

"Are you here for the talent show?" His father spoke the words very sharply. He looked upset.

"No, I'm not here about the contest or the talent show. I'm here just to talk, to see how you are doing."

His father's face relaxed. He stared at the Guru attentively.

"Do you know who I am?" The Guru asked quietly.

"I'll know if you tell me."

"I'm your son. *Harris.*" The Guru leaned forward in his chair.

"Sure you are. I know you all right. I know you went to California."

"That's right. I went to California after college. After DeKalb. A long time ago."

"Northern Illinois University," his father said.

"That's right," said the Guru. "A long time ago."

"How is California?"

"I don't live in California any more. I haven't lived there for a long time. Do you remember that I live in Colorado sometimes? That I live in the Caribbean sometimes? On an island? On a little island called Heart's Rest?"

His father looked unhappy, lost.

"I do. I live in Colorado sometimes and other times on an island in the Bahamas. You probably don't remember because I travel quite a bit. I travel all over the world. Do you remember the things I sent you? Do you remember the pictures? The books?"

"No."

The Guru looked about the room. On his father's bureau he recognized a framed photograph of himself at the Star Shower Cascade. In the photograph he was standing at the Altar of Sharing overlooking the Great Vale. His arms were raised high, his head was thrown back, and his smiling face was bright with sunlight. The Guru retrieved the framed picture from the bureau and brought it for his father to see.

"Here I am," he said. "Here I am in Colorado."

His father looked at the photograph for a moment then put it face down in his lap. His expression relaxed into a slow smile.

"Harris," he said.

"Yes," said the Guru, smiling now himself.

For a moment his father's eyes were fixed on the Guru's robe. At length he said, "You've gotten big. Like your mother."

"Yes," the Guru said softly.

"You know she had terrible, terrible asthma."

"Yes, I know."

They sat in silence for several minutes. The Guru thought his father looked delicate and very beautiful under the sunlit billows of his green shirt. His father closed his eyes, and the Guru thought he might be asleep, but he opened them again, raised the photograph from his lap and gave it a long, considered look.

"Put this back," he said.

The Guru placed the photograph back on the bureau. The louvered door to his father's closet was slightly ajar, and the Guru pulled it open to look. The suits and sports jackets were hung neatly on specially molded wooden hangers. Next his newly creased trousers were hung from the cuffs. Next to them was a line of freshly laundered dress shirts and sports shirts. Everything was clean, seemingly new. The Guru was about to close the closet door when he saw, suspended by two brass brackets, the tie rack he had made for his father in Junior High. The bright blue figures of the blue jay—the school mascot—was perched on a white painted dowel rod over which were draped his father's ties. To the Guru's eyes, the tie rack was just as he had made it. The blue feathers, the yellow beak, the white perch gleamed brilliantly under the shellac. Tears welled in the Guru's yes.

"You have the old tie rack," he said, closing the closet door.

"Yes," said his father, "for my ties."

The receptionist was standing in the open doorway. "Dinner time." She said to the Guru's father, then, turning to the Guru, "Are you sure you can't stay?"

"No. Thank you."

"Well, I'm sure you had a lovely, a very nice visit."

"He travels," Otto Mueller said with sudden force, "all over the world."

12

The Fat Piece of Shit

The featureless, low-slung neighborhoods of Schaumberg eventually gave way to a tangle of intersections overhung with closely spaced traffic lights.

"Rush hour," Forrester said. "Our best bet is the toll way."

"Yes," the Guru said absently. It seemed to him that the car had not moved for a long time. Out the windows on either side the other cars, the same cars, idled in their fumes. *Rush hour.* The Guru lay his head back on the seat and closed his eyes.

He saw the tie rack, the sheen of the blue jay perched on the white dowel, at the back of his father's closet. He remembered the jolt, the sinking feeling of loss when Mr. Bianchi, the sour-faced shop teacher, handed him his project with an index card taped to the blue jay. Mr. Bianchi had said only his name, *Mueller*, and handed him the tie rack. On the card he had written: *Neat work. You missed some steps. Edges not sanded—B.* It was true, he had not rounded the edges of the figure of the jay after Mr. Bianchi had cut it out on the jigsaw. Even under the heavy enamel paint and shellac, he could see a fine fringe, like hair, where the blade had cut the pine. Alone, at his locker, the card—the <u>B</u>—made him cry. A <u>B</u> wasn't good in shop.

Remembering, the Guru felt the sadness and hopelessness tighten around his heart. P.J. Peterson had seen him bent into his locker, sobbing.

"What's the matter, Mueller? Are you *crying*?" P. J. Peterson was one of the popular boys. The Guru wanted him to pass on, to leave him alone, but he stood there behind him, practically touching him.

"Leave me alone," the Guru said without turning around.

P.J. Peterson grabbed the shoulder of his shirt and pulled him away from the locker.

"You're *crying*, Mueller. What are you crying about?" Then, to the cluster of other boys who had gathered: "Mueller's crying. What's wrong, Mueller?"

The Guru tried to pry P.J. Peterson's fingers away from the shoulder of his shirt, but he couldn't.

"Let go of my shirt." The Guru's eyes were hot and blurred with tears. His throat was swollen with shame and sadness. He sensed a darkness, a terrible void opening up just behind him. He could fall back into it. He could die. *I might have to die.*

"I will when I feel like it," P. J. Peterson said. "I will when you tell me why you're crying."

The Guru experienced the Feeling. He moved in close to P.J. Peterson, his mouth and nose close enough to kiss him. The Guru drew up the corners of his mouth in an exaggerated smile.

"You smell bad," he said.

The other boys hooted and laughed.

P. J. Peterson released his hold on his shirt and shoved him roughly back into the locker face.

"What was that, Mueller? What did you say to me?"

"You heard me."

"Yeah, Mueller, I heard you."

The Guru had an impression of P.J. Peterson's teeth. He saw P. J. Peterson's eyes go vacant, and then, with a terrible clarity, he felt the slap. Blood red, ringing, like a shout.

The Guru closed his eyes on the tears. He drew up the corners of his mouth and held the smile.

"You like that, Mueller?" he heard P. J. Peterson say. "You like that, you fat piece of shit?"

The next slap was like a flash of yellow light behind the Guru's tightly squeezed lids. But he had already started to fall back into the void. Someone was saying, as if from a great distance, "Leave him alone, P.J."

Then P. J. Peterson's voice was right in his ear, like a hiss, like a roar.

"Because that's what you are, blubber lips. You are nothing but a fat piece of shit."

13
The T.B. Test

The concerned look in Granny Mueller's eyes made him feel ashamed and sad.

"Did something happen? Has something *happened* at school?" she asked him.

He said no, he was just sick.

"But Harris you can't be sick everyday." She put her palm to his forehead, which he knew would be cool.

Walking in the morning to the Junior High he felt the mounting weight in his stomach, the thickening in his throat, and he had to breathe hard not to cry. Once inside the building and moving through the tiled hallways smelling of wax and student lunches, he would draw the darkness over his head and shoulders like a shawl. He had learned to hear and not to hear, to see and not to see. He practiced Stillness: standing still as others moved about him on the playground or in the cafeteria, sitting still at his desk. He wanted to perfect his stillness, to become like glass, transparent, invisible.

In homeroom Mr. Franklin's announcement of the T.B. test dissolved his stillness. It did not seem possible that they would do it, that they would do it to every student in the school. It was because Mr. Calderone, the eighth grade math teacher, got T.B. and had to go to a sanitarium.

Mr. Franklin said they should not worry. He said there was no danger. He said he had been tested already himself and that it was nothing. There was a little tine—*tine*—which was treated with a preparation that showed if T.B. bacilli had ever entered your system. The nurse would prick the skin of your forearm with the tine. It would feel like a tickle, a scratch. It was nothing, Mr. Franklin said again.

The Guru felt his heart beating in his throat. *No. There must be no tine, no prick of T.B. in the skin of my arm.* He heard and did not hear Caroline McKee say, "I heard it really *hurts.*" He heard and did not hear Mr. Franklin explaining that the test could be positive or negative and that probably all of them would be negative, that negative was good.

This was Tuesday, and the test would be Friday. He would be sick on Friday, but this plan did not make him feel better. He imagined the tuberculosis bacilli, emerging like tiny brown crabs from the pointed tine. A nurse was lowering the gleaming tine down toward the soft skin of his forearm. The Guru felt an icy sensation at the back of his neck. *I don't have to. I won't.*

Thursday night as he was drying the dishes after supper the Guru told Granny Mueller he felt sick, but she did not look concerned. She looked hard into his eyes, and then her face relaxed.

"Harris, I think you are going to be just fine. And you just ate a nice big supper."

It was true. He had eaten everything.

In the morning, he came to the table in his pajamas, not his school clothes. "I'm really sick," he said. "I feel like throwing up."

Granny Mueller clapped her palm over his forehead, then the back of his neck. She clasped both of his wrists.

"Harris Mueller," she said. "You are fine. You are absolutely fine, and you are going to school. Now go into your room and get dressed. You're going to be late. *March.*"

That morning Granny Mueller walked him to the edge of the playground on her way to the bakery.

Inside the school the Guru thought he really might be going to throw up. He heard a ringing, hissing sound in his ears as he sat down to home room as he waited, clenching and unclenching his hands, for the class to be led away for the test. But Mr. Franklin began reviewing the homework questions on *Johnny Tremain*, and after the first bell, he handed out the *Road to Independence* books for Silent Reading. He did not mention the T.B. test.

The Guru felt a wonderful relief, an all-being restfulness. Then the school nurse poked her head in the door and said "all set" to Mr. Franklin.

"All right, folks, leave your books as they are, and stand, please. We are going to walk *single file*..."

The Guru stood but did not stand. He experienced the first eruption of The Force of No.

His section met an already waiting line of fifty or sixty boys and girls. Where the far end of the corridor opened up to the lobby of the gym, the Guru could see two uniformed nurses leading students behind a temporary partition. The line progressed very slowly, and he heard and did not hear his classmates chattering in front of him and behind him. Every minute or so a boy or girl released from the testing stations would pass by on the other side of the corridor. The Guru heard and did not hear Caroline McKee hiss, "Didn't hurt at *all*," as she passed.

When there were only four students ahead of him, the Guru made a low hum in his throat. He wanted to run past the testing stations to the gym lobby doors and run home, but he would have to pass the nurses and teachers, and they would catch him. The hum was louder, and, hearing and not hearing someone say "next," he left the line and began walking back toward the home room.

"*Mueller*, where are you going?"

"Mueller, it's your *turn*."

He had not perfected walking and not walking. He called prayerfully on the Stillness.

He had nearly reached the back of the line when he was stopped by a firm yet gentle hand on his shoulder. It was Mr. Franklin.

"Harris," he said, "Where are you going?"

"Home."

Mr. Franklin led him farther along the corridor, away from the other children.

"Harris, what do you mean you're going home? You can't go home. Without telling anybody. What's wrong? Is it the test? Are you afraid?"

The Guru heard and did not hear.

"Are you afraid of the test?"

The Guru was humming again, and when he could not make it loud enough, he began to breathe very hard, but this broke apart into heaving, sputtering sobs.

Mr. Franklin bent over him, held him. The Guru entered the darkness of his jacket, entered it like night.

The Guru heard and did not hear the other children as they passed by after their tests. He heard and did not hear, saw but did not see the rest of the morning. He was allowed to sit by himself in the quiet of the nurse's office. Afterward the nurse walked with him to the cafeteria. Then he was standing still on the playground.

"*Mueller*," P.J. Peterson was saying, "Why didn't you take the test? What's the matter, can't you talk? Were you too scared to take the test? Is that why you were crying? You cry a lot, Harris. You know that, Harris? You know why, Harris? I'll tell you why. It's because you're a *fairy*, Harris. You are. You're a fairy. *Harry the fairy*."

The Guru did not move. He heard but did not hear.

14

The Guru Bi-Locates

On a clear and cool Saturday morning not long after the T.B. test, the Guru experienced the Rapture in the Trees.

Granny Mueller had asked him to help her clean out the gutters. For this he had to climb up the stepladder from the back porch to the low slanting roof over the shed at the rear of the garage. From there he could creep over the pebbly shingles to the roof of the house.

Granny Mueller handed up a tin bucket, a trowel, and an old pair of cloth garden gloves. He guided the pail handle up into the crook of his arm and stepped gingerly up to where the chimney emerged from the peak. A gust swooshed and rattled in the elms on either side.

"Harris. Harris?" Granny Mueller had backed up to the Kendall hedge in order to see him. "Harris, now why don't you sit down and scoot on your bottom down to where you can reach the gutters. Very, very careful. Over here. We'll start in this corner."

It made his stomach go light to inch down toward the edge of the roof of the bungalow, but when his sneakers neared the gutter line he could see Granny Mueller, and her head was only a few feet below him. *It would not be far to fall.*

His job was to scoop out the soggy dead leaves and silt from the gutter with the trowel. In some places, the debris had compacted into a kind of tangy soil in which elm seeds had taken root. When he could not pull it up with a trowel, he pried it up with his gloved hand. When the bucket was full, he dumped it out onto the ground below where Granny Mueller raked it up into her garden cart.

After a while, Granny Mueller said that if he was all right up there, she would look after a few things she needed to do in the house.

The Guru felt happy and at rest inching his bottom over the shingles, scooping up the brown gunk into the bucket. It pleased him to see the clear contrast between the empty trough he had cleaned and the unaddressed mulch in front of him.

It did not seem a long time before Granny Mueller called him inside for lunch. "You are such a help!" She told him. He knew that she was glad. She gave him a BLT on white toast, potato chips, and a Pepsi. The moist and salty BLT was delicious on his tongue, and Granny Mueller made him another.

"Back to the salt mines," she said when he had finished.

That afternoon when he was only a few feet from the last downspout on the street end of the house, he felt an uncomfortable cramping behind his knees. He did not want to finish the job feeling this way so he rose slowly to stretch. He took off the gloves and placed them with the trowel in the bucket. Then he turned, inclining forward so that his fingertips grazed the shingles, and made his way up to the chimney. Bracing himself against the brickwork he planted both feet on the spine of the roof.

Looking straight ahead, he saw only leaves, a medium of elm and maple. The breeze was steady now, and the branches rose and fell slightly, and the Guru imagined the leafy boughs were great mattresses of feathers, that he could lie out and sink into them as they rose and fell. He heard the clout of a screen door slamming shut and looked down to see Emily Kendall and a friend hurry down the front steps and turn down the street toward town. The breeze dispersed the gabble of their talk as they made their way, purses bobbing against their backs. They did not see him. He knew no one could see him.

The Guru stood away from the chimney. He extended his arms on either side and closed his eyes. He held the picture of the racks of leaves, greenly rising and falling like feathers, like plumes under the glass blue sky. The Guru listened. The breeze moving through the leaves was like voices, like sighs of pleasure. He opened his eyes, and he could see the crystalline dance of the air between the shivering leaves and his face. The leaves, the excited air, the shingles, the rubber soles of his sneakers, his socks, his skin, his swelling heart, his tingling palms were all held in it, all moving with it. *Everything touches.* And the Guru could not bear it. He threw his head back and felt the current drop from his skull and shudder along his spine.

I am always here. This is mine.

At the Junior High he was saved only by the Stillness.

With the cooler weather, the co-recreation classes moved indoors, to the gym and the cafeteria where Coach Laughlin presided over Square Dancing. The Guru sat down with the others, seeing and not seeing, hearing and not hearing, as Coach Laughlin used P.J. Peterson and Stephanie Minton to demonstrate the swing, the do-si-do, the promenade. Stephanie Minton's face and neck were blotched with red blushes, and P.J. Peterson made faces to his friends as he and Stephanie orbited each other in the figures of the Square Dance.

"All right, *gentlemen.*" Coach Laughlin said loudly, "Choose your partner."

The Guru sensed the void just behind him. He would not think, he would not feel. He moved through the confusion of boys and girls until he spotted Sissy Fisk. Sissy Fisk had been his partner in Art. She did not speak. He spotted the fuzz of her pale hair, but she was standing opposite Ellis Miller. She had been picked. He heard his own low hum begin in his throat. *It doesn't matter.* He wheeled abruptly and tapped the shoulder of the first white blouse.

Trish Goodman, surprised, turned and looked at him with angry disbelief. Her mouth opened, but for a moment she did not speak.

"*What?*" she demanded.

The Guru's ears were ringing. Trish Goodman was one of the popular girls. She looked very tall standing close to him. He could feel the tension of her anger.

"I choose you," he said.

"Oh—*peachy!*" Trish Goodman turned back to her friends, but they had been picked and were being led away.

Coach Laughlin blew his whistle. "O.K.," he said, "Everybody got a partner? *Good.* O.K., everybody make a circle and join hands."

The Guru and Trish Goodman backed into what was becoming a circle.

"And join hands," said Coach Laughlin again.

Without looking, the Guru knew that Trish Goodman was staring straight ahead of her and that she was mad. Without looking, he found her hand with his. He closed his fingers over the back of her hand, but she straightened her fingers rigidly. She would not clasp his hand. Feeling and not feeling, the Guru closed his grip around her wrist.

After co-recreational Square Dancing, and after he ate his lunch in Stillness, the Guru stepped out onto the playground. He looked reflexively for a group to stand near, to hear and not hear. The boys were fanned out over the outfield of the ball diamond idly kicking a ball from one to the other. The girls stood talking in clusters behind the backstop. He would take a walk. He would circle around the baseball diamond, encircling all of them.

As he approached the backstop he heard it.

Trish Goodman's back was to him and the other girls were leaning into her. He heard her high whining voice.

"And then I get to dance with Harry the Fairy!"

He heard and did not hear the other girls shush Trish Goodman. He heard and did not hear one of them say, "He's right *behind* you."

The air between him and the girls was stinging and prickly like bits of glass.

The Guru walked home. Until Granny Mueller returned from the bakery at five, he sat in the stillness of the shadowy living room.

"Sorry about this," Forrester was saying.

The Guru had drawn deeply into his interior, but he was aware that he should answer.

"Excuse me," he said, "What are you sorry about?"

"The traffic. I thought going back into the city, we'd miss some of the rush hour. We're just crawling."

The Guru saw the sun reflecting whitely on the cars crowded in close around the Town Car. Exhaust fumes made the light seem to wriggle against the pale horizon. *Like a prison.*

Weakly, heavily, the Guru felt himself descend back into the Sadness of Junior High. He seemed to hover just above his own shoulders as he sat bent over his home room desk, scripting his name slowly and perfectly, scripting it backwards, *Sirrah Relleum.*

In June, on one of the last days before being released for the summer, he experienced the first bi-location. There was an extended period of Phys. Ed. Because of the hot weather. Coach Nettis had called the names Peterson and Morganti, named them Captains, and told them to pick teams for softball.

"Come on, Tony, P.J.," Coach Nettis said, "Heads or tails for first pick. You call it, P. J."

The Guru did not have a glove. You needed a glove to catch hard throws and ground balls and fly balls. The rubber-coated softball would bend back your fingers, make your palms sting. He saw and did not see the faces of the other boys waiting behind the backstop to be picked. The Guru entered the Stillness. Because he was left standing apart, looking and not looking at the boys shuffling around P.J. Peterson and Tony Morganti, he knew he would be picked last and that being last could be part of the Stillness. Neither boy called his name. Coach Nettis had said "O.K., and Mueller, you're with Morganti. Let's play ball."

The sides were uneven. Tony Morganti had nine players, P.J. Peterson only eight. Since Coach Nettis pitched for both sides, there was an extra player on Tony Morganti's team.

"The sides are uneven. We have an extra player," the Guru said softly to Coach Nettis, as his side bickered for positions in the field. "I'll watch."

"*Watch?*" Coach Nettis smiled kindly, "No watching in baseball, Harris. Let's see." Coach Nettis scanned the field behind him. "O.K., here we go, we got a hole in right-center field. You're our right-center fielder today. O.K.? Let's *play ball.*"

The Guru knew right-center field was not a position.

"Not fair," someone called out as he trotted to the outfield. "They got four outfielders."

"No big deal," P.J. Peterson said, "It's just Mueller."

"Play ball."

The first pitch was hit sharply over the second baseman's head. The Guru sensed the inevitability. Before it bounced on the hard turf, he had seen it coming straight toward his heart. He felt a weak, helpless tingling in his belly and behind his knees. He would not be able to catch the ball when it came to him. He would extend his bare hands stiffly and it would buzz stingingly through his fingers. The game would begin with his error. The game would begin with nagging complaints.

The Guru left the Stillness. He decided to charge the ball, do whatever was to be done as quickly and forcefully as he could. The first bounce was head high. The second, when the Guru charged to meet it, skidded low over the grass. As the Guru bent at the waist to grab it, the ball kicked up over his wrists and struck him numbingly below his mouth. The impact made his teeth click together. There was an impression of desperate running, of much shouting in the infield. "Throw it in, Mueller!" "Second." "He's going for *second!*" The ball had come to rest just behind him. "Come *on*, Mueller!" The Guru picked up the softball and threw it as far as he could in the direction of Coach Nettis.

The play and the shouting and the raised dust were all in the infield. The Guru back-pedaled far into right-center field. His eyes were clouded with tears, and the skin between his chin and lower lip buzzed like a bee.

Coach Nettis was ready to pitch again. He turned to right center field and called out, "Everything OK out there, Mueller? Everything OK? That was a nice stop."

The Guru was deep in Stillness when it was his turn to bat.

"Come on, Mueller," someone was saying. "Two outs. Please don't whiff."

The Guru rested the fat black bat on his shoulder and peered out to Coach Nettis on the mound. Coach Nettis looked at him kindly. The pitch made a slow arc well above his head and then dropped to the level of his face when he lifted the bat to meet it. The bat just grazed the rubber cover of the ball.

"O.K., Harris," Coach Nettis said, "Keep your eye on it."

The Guru had seen it, had seen it perfectly.

The next pitch was higher still, and he could not reach it with his bat. He heard and did not hear the complaints and the joking.

"Bad pitch, Harris," Coach Nettis said. Wait for a strike."

The Guru waited. The next pitch was familiar, like the first but it would drop lower, closer to his waist. The Guru drew the bat back and, as he swung it around, closed his eyes.

"Oh *god*," a voice said behind him.

"Harris," Coach Nettis said as the fielders ran in to bat, "You've got to do more than wave the bat."

The Guru was hurt, startled.

"What?"

"You're just waving the bat."

At first he could not reach the Stillness. He was aware only of the hot, dusty ball field and the effort to make his legs carry him out to right center field. The sunlight on the browning grass was harsh and relentless, and he felt a sickening weakness. It was true. He had only waved the bat. It might have been an umbrella or a long useless feather.

The Guru back-pedaled deep into the outfield. He heard and didn't hear someone way, "Hey, Mueller, where are you going?" The brown grass had grown deep and lush, and as he extended his arms wide, there was only shivering green, the green leaves of the elms, and the sighs of pleasure were steadily louder and more beckoning, and his feet were planted firmly on the ridge pole of Granny Mueller's roof, and once again he could see the very air.

15
The Salvation of Perfection

The Town Car pulled under the awning of the Sheraton, and as Forrester opened the door for the Guru, Kamala and Andy-dam met them on the walk.

Did you have a good day?" Andy-dam asked.

The Guru clapped his hands heavily on Andy-dam's shoulders and smiled. "I've had many days."

Kamala led the Guru inside. Andy-dam settled with Forrester, who explained the delay was due to the surprising traffic returning to the city. Andy-dam sensed that Forrester was reluctant to get back into the car.

"Exactly what kind of...religion is it?" Forrester asked.

"It is not a religion," Andy-dam explained. "It is an approach to life that draws on many religious teachings, eastern and western. It is about living more completely, more deeply. The Master is our spiritual teacher."

"How do people—" Forrester hesitated. "How do you get the word out?"

"That is interesting," Andy-dam said warmly. "Basically, it just happens. It started when people had important personal encounters with the Master. They would hear his Teachings. Or they might read one of his published writings. There are directed courses of study and meditations. There are now several meditation centers. And we have a web site."

Forrester looked thoughtful. He showed no sign of wanting to get into the car.

"Would you like some information about the Movement?" Andy-dam asked.

"Yes, I would. Thank you."

Andy-dam excused himself and left Forrester on the walk in the muggy evening air. Forrester gazed about absently at the distant masses of the other hotels. The sky overhead was the color of the pavement.

In a minute Andy-dam returned with two tri-fold brochures, "Invitation to Reality" and "Who is the Master?" and a copy of the monograph *Heart's Call*.

"Here you are. The Master thanks you especially for your patience and kind consideration." Andy-dam shook Forrester's hand. "Perhaps we will see you again."

The Guru stepped out of his sandals and *lhoti* and moved to the bed which had been turned down earlier by the Sheraton staff. Kamala chided him for having eaten nothing since his morning juice. Without appetite he eyed the prepared tray of curried vegetables over rice, the bottle of distilled water, the orange juice. He felt heavy, bloated. He raised his arms high over his head, inhaled and exhaled deeply.

"Are you all right?" Kamala asked.

"Oh, yes." Then brightly: "I have always been all right—and you, for that matter, have always been all right. It is just that today I decided to reenter the perfect silliness of my childhood."

"Was your childhood silly?"

"Yes, my love. It was brutally silly."

Lying back naked on top of the cool sheets, the Guru opened his eyes wide to the surrounding darkness.

He had meant to pass by the High School. More massive, older, heavier in its stones, the High School had given him room. He recalled the quiet, the thickly bound books that were his to take home. In High School he had embraced the pleasure of Perfection.

Perfection had dissolved the heaviness of the hours. He no longer heard the distinct clicking of the minutes on the classroom clocks. The Perfection had begun with his notebook, newly purchased for High School. On the bottom of the inside cover, he had made a dark line in ball-point over his ruler. With great care, he scripted his name. *Sirrah Relleum*, perfectly. With the same care he then inscribed onto the manila tabs of the dividers the names of his subjects: English, Algebra, World History, Physical Science, and Latin. He slid a full package of ruled notebook paper over the rings between each divider, a full package for each subject.

At the start of each class, he would use the small plastic ruler from his pencil case to make a new line near the top upper right-hand margin of the paper, and he would enter the day's date, slowly, perfectly. He took notes in Outline Form, carefully considering which of the teacher's points were Topics and which were Subordinate. At his desk in his room at home, he would center his notebook on the blotter, line up his sharpened pencils and the ball-point to the right of the blotter. On the shelf at the back of his desk he would stack his books, the spines facing him in the order he would use them. If he made an error or had to rework a homework problem, he would neatly re-copy the page. He took exquisite care composing and recopying graphs. Mr. Fiedler had held up his first laboratory report in front of the class.

Lying in the dark, the Guru felt a pleasing lightening in his midsection as he recalled these early perfections. Granny Mueller would look into his room after supper, linger in the doorway. She would say, "Harris, you are such a *scholar.*" He savored the slowness, the effort at perfection. He pressed the ridged pencils down hard so that the elegant numbers and rounded zeroes were clear and dark. He pressed the ballpoint down so that the sentences and outline entries made deep indentations into the paper.

The last thing he did before leaving his desk to brush his teeth was to leaf back over the pages of his notebook to the beginning. There was a gratifying bulk to the inscribed pages, soon too many to count, line after line, sheet after ruled sheet of his findings, his notes, his accumulated work, scripted perfectly. The effort had made the illusion of effort dissolve, had made the illusion of Time dissolve.

The Guru felt himself dropping agreeably into sleep when he remembered the still greater pleasure of Ann Frank.

When Mrs. Sinsheimer handed out the glossy paperback copies of *The Diary of Ann Frank,* there was a distinctly charged atmosphere in the classroom. Some of the other students knew about the book. It was about Jewish families hiding from the Nazis in Amsterdam in World War II. The Nazis would find them and send them to the concentration camps. It was a true story. Ann Frank died.

The Guru had pictured an old fashioned city in Europe. He saw lines of soldiers marching in the rain. He imagined a highly particular dullness, like the images in magazines stacked in the garage, like history.

But almost from the outset *The Diary of Ann Frank* was not like that, was not at all like history. Ann was irresistibly friendly and lively. Her diary charged the air. The Guru could sometimes read no more than a page or two without closing the book again to study the drawing of Ann on the cover. He was fascinated by the dark, recessed orbits of her eyes, the liveliness—but also the seriousness—of the narrow face. The Guru imagined living quietly and intensely with the Franks in their secret room upstairs behind the false wall. There would be no High School, no Phys. Ed., no entering the Stillness in the cafeteria. Peter would be his friend, but Ann would be his best friend. He knew she would like him enormously. They would wake up in the morning excited to see each other. Ann was so generous and kind, even when she thought about the people outside of the house. He and Ann would gather blankets and cushions and huddle together in a quiet corner of the attic. The light outside the shuttered window was grimy and grey, like history, but it was wonderful to be near it, huddled next to Ann. He imagined reading her diary not at his desk in the house on West Walnut but huddled next to Ann in the attic. Then he would show her his Note Book.

The Guru had not wanted to finish *The Diary of Ann Frank*. It made him feel weak and deeply sad to see there were only a few pages left, just a sliver of paper pinched between his thumb and forefinger. Her diary, the real diary would, he knew, be scripted beautifully. He was aware also that Ann Frank somehow really did know him and knew how much he loved her. Ann Frank was a perfection.

16
Tears of Blood

At four a.m. the Guru awoke and did not know where he was. An alarmed, queasy feeling, a feeling he had not experienced for a long time, descended from the base of his throat to his belly. He beheld a loose succession of images from the day before: Palatine, his father. He tried to form an image of Ann Frank, but the pleasure did not arrive. Then, sickeningly, he recalled the sweater.

Granny Mueller had always given him an allowance, but as he was about to enter his sophomore year, she surprised him by increasing it from twelve dollars a month to twenty-five. The sum had taken him by surprise. He pictured a crisp twenty-dollar bill and a five -dollar bill in his billfold. It was more than he would ever spend.

"You can start saving," Granny Mueller told him. "You can learn to make a budget."

Part of her plan in increasing his allowance was to make him responsible for personal expenses, including some of his clothes, movies and magazines and sweets.

His first unguided purchase had been a crewneck sweater. Still operating under his Learner's Permit, he drove with Granny Mueller in the Ford to J.C. Penney's Department Store. He told his grandmother they should meet back at the car in half an hour; he had an errand he wanted to do.

In the Boys and Men's Department, he made his way to the sweaters. There was a look he had come to like in the high school, especially among the taller, leaner upper classmen. They wore dark crew neck sweaters which showed a little of the collar of a white shirt above the stitching of the neck. The Guru thought the crew neck sweaters showing a white stripe of collar created a clean, priestly look. The older boys in their crew neck sweaters moving briskly through the corridors between classes looked comfortable, well dressed, just right.

The Guru did not at first see any crew necks. He held up some of the sweaters to look at them, but they had vee-necks or rounded necks. There were stacks of vests and cardigans. A floor assistant asked if he needed help, and he said he wanted a crewneck sweater. He was taken to a counter stacked with sweaters that had the stitched necks of the crew-necked sweaters he knew, but they were mottled with bright colors or they were cut through with stripes. Some of them were patterned with snowflakes or snowmen. These, the assistant said, were "holiday sweaters." The Guru began to lose confidence. He asked if there were any plain ones. The assistant picked out a few that were mostly one color, but there was a band of another color around the neck or the waistband. Uncomfortably, the Guru studied a bright red sweater with black trim at the collar and waist. "It's a crew neck," the assistant said. At length the Guru said no, he did not want a red one. The assistant invited him to look around and left him alone. He wanted a black sweater or a dark blue one, but there were none stacked on the shelves. He looked at his watch. Twenty minutes had passed. But as he began to walk out of Boys and Men's, he felt an unpleasant weight of failure in his stomach. *It is just a sweater.* He made his way back to the stacks of patterned crew-neck sweaters. He spotted at the bottom of one of the piles a promising expanse of soft grey wool. He pried it out from under the others and held it up to look. He felt a stab of disappointment. The grey was only a broad stripe in a banded series of other stripes— blue, brown, tan—that rose up the length of the sweater. "Find something you like?" The attendant had returned. "Why not try it on?"

In the full length mirror he saw that the sweater did not create the crewneck sweater look. The broad stripes seemed to expand in width as they passed over his stomach so that his mid-section looked swollen. As he looked at himself under the fluorescent light, the stripes seemed to move a little where one color met the next. "That's a very nice weave," the attendant was saying. "That's mohair." *Hair.* The sweater was like a fine soft hair, like the hair of a kitten. The collar of his plaid shirt did not look right at the neck. It would look different, better with his white shirt. He remembered the time. Thirty minutes had passed.

The sweater cost fourteen ninety-five, and the Guru paid with the twenty dollar bill from his allowance. He pictured himself, perfectly, walking between classes in the striped crew neck. He was wearing his white shirt. *It will be the look I have.*

"Stripes!" Granny Mueller said when he took it out of the bag to show her in the car. "Now that's an interesting sweater. "And," she said feeling it, "so nice and soft."

The sweater, he realized when he studied it in the bathroom mirror when he got home, was not right, but it was fascinating. Granny Mueller said it was nice, a perfect fit. In his mind's eye, as he lay in bed, he saw the stripes expanding enormously over his belly.

Without actually hearing them, the Guru knew the girls behind him in Physical Science were talking about him. He heard one of them say "Cheshire cat." He heard "raccoon." There was an awful excitement in the cadence of their whispering, now and then a strangled squeal. He dreaded the bell, his exposure to them in the cafeteria.

He felt the bell's metallic pulsing in the center of his chest. He sat still at his seat as the other students gathered up their books, exploded noisily into chatter.

He was aware of a presence behind him.

"Harris," Donna Degregorio said with a nervous brightness. "Look at your notes. The *writing*. Oh my god, it's so *perfect*."

The Guru closed his notebook. Debbie Holmes and Katie Glaser had joined Donna Degregorio. The three girls crowded in close around the aisle side of his desk, making it awkward for him to rise.

"Can I show them?" Donna Degregorio asked.

"I want to see," said Katie Glaser.

The Guru knew they were mocking him.

"You want to see my notes," he said evenly. He opened his notebook.

"Oh my god, they are. They're so perfect."

"They're so neat."

The Guru waited until the girls exited the science room before gathering up his things. The girls had lingered just up the corridor and stole glances at him as he passed. He was aware of them not far behind him as he approached the cafeteria. He heard an eruption of shrill giggles. He heard "*dare* you." He heard "*No!*" There was more laughter, and then Donna Degregorio was walking at his side.

"Harris," she said, "I hope this doesn't seem too forward of a question"--she made a snuffle of laughter, then covered her mouth—"*but*, we were wondering…I was wondering whether sometime, sometime when you're not *using* it, if one of us could borrow your sweater."

He did not turn to look at Donna Degregorio. He was aware only that she had dropped back from his side and that her voice was mingled with the muffled laughter of her friends.

The Guru listened for the flush of the toilet, the closing and click of Granny Mueller's bedroom door. He crept on the balls of his feet down the hall to the back bathroom, quietly closed and locked the door behind him. He stared hard into the mirror above the sink. In a few seconds his image grew indistinct, and he saw only the sweater, the bands of stripes vibrating busily in the buttery fluorescence. He raised his arms, and the striped convexity of his torso looked clown-like. He looked hugely fat. He reached a hand behind him and pulled the sweater tight around his belly. *I am. I am fat.*

The Guru felt a welcome passivity, a dullness. He pulled the sweater up over his head and stepped out of the rest of his clothes. He opened the mirrored door of the medicine cabinet and took out Granny Mueller's nail scissors. Holding down the waistband of the sweater under his knee and stretching out the fabric with his left hand, he was able to cut the body of the sweater up to the neck. The Guru cut the striped sweater into little squares of grey and blue and brown and tan wool. He realized it was late, but he felt less tired than in a kind of trance of passivity.

Standing at the mirror, he considered the milky expanse of his chest and stomach. Not looking at his skin, but at its reflection in the mirror over the sink, he pricked the pointed tip of the nail scissors into the flesh above his right nipple. He watched as a small rounded bead of dark blood formed over the puncture. Still in the grip of the calmness, feeling somehow afloat, the Guru scratched a curved bracket on each side of the puncture. Dreamily, he punctured and bracketed the skin over his left nipple. By early morning the pattern had formed exquisitely downward from his collarbone to the arc defining his rib cage. The beads of blood from the punctures darkened from viscous red to purple and black as they hardened. *Like tears*, he realized. *My ancient tears of blood.*

He had not wanted to shower at all after Phys. Ed. But Coach Atkinson had seen him at his locker pulling his slacks up over his gym shorts. "Everybody showers, Mueller," he said. "We had a real workout today."

He used the urinal, washed his hands, stalled and lingered as long as he could while the other boys returned from their showers and dressed. Finally, turning in toward his open locker he pulled off his gym shirt and quickly draped his towel over his shoulders, holding the ends tight to his chest. He was relieved to find himself alone in the shower room, but as he turned off the taps and reached for his towel, Coach Atkinson stood framed in the entrance.

"Mueller, what is *that*?" He pulled the Guru's arms away from his chest. "What the hell have you done to yourself?"

Granny Mueller was not reachable when the school nurse called her at the bakery. The assistant principal had to call his father, and it took him more than an hour to get to the High School from the south side of the city.

"What did you do, Harris? Did you cut yourself?"

His father looked embarrassed, uncomfortable sitting with the nurse and the assistant principal.

"Harris," the nurse said, "I think you should show your father your chest. We can step out."

"I'll show him at home," the Guru said.

His father was wearing his green golf shirt under his overcoat, not a suit and tie.

The nurse gave his father the slip with the number of the doctor they were supposed to call. His father had not known what to say. He said, "Thanks for everything."

Outside on the way to the car, his father said, "Harris, what did you do?"

The Guru saw that his father was about to cry.

17

The Guru Resolves to Share

The Guru rose from his meditation mat at the foot of his bed and, still in his *lhoti*, left the bedroom to rouse the others.

Over juice and tea and yogurt he announced to Andy-dam, Kamala, and Curtis Forbes that he would resume the Sharings when they returned to Star Shower.

"When you are rested," Curtis Forbes said.

"I would like to start," the Guru said, "immediately."

"But the doctors at the clinic said to rest. They said for a week or two. Then they wanted to check your response to the medicines."

"Sharing," the Guru said, "Will be my rest."

"We are due in tonight," said Andy-dam. "Tomorrow is Friday. When would you like to start?"

"As soon as possible. Immediately. By the weekend, if we can." The Guru smiled broadly. He clasped his hands behind his neck and threw back his head.

"I will post a session on the web site," Andy-dam said. "You know we are going to be heavily subscribed. It's been a while."

Kamala caught the Guru's eye across the table. "You definitely feel strong enough?"

"Of course I do, my love." The Guru was happy, exuberant. "Strong like bull!" The Guru laughed.

Andy-dam leaned forward. "So a Sharing, one Sharing, to start as soon as we can get a response, which could be as soon as this weekend, or Monday? You would like me to post it?"

"Post *them*."

"Sorry?"

"Post *them*," said the Guru. "There will be a *series* of Sharings. A series of three."

Andy-dam looked concerned. "One each month?"

"No," said the Guru. "Let's make them as continuous as possible, with only the time it takes in between to clean the rooms."

"That doesn't give the Internationals much time to book travel."

The Guru considered. "Not for the first one, certainly. But where there is heart, a trip can be arranged in a week. It can be arranged in an hour."

Andy-dam's face clouded. He thought about the extra expense of plane tickets purchased on short notice.

Curtis Forbes said, "This is important, isn't it?"

"Of course it is." The Guru was beaming, his eyes wide with humor. "We only do what is important."

Andy-dam excused himself to boot up his laptop. The Guru took Kamala's hand in his and with his other hand reached across to clasp Curtis Forbes'. "You have been wonderfully kind and patient in indulging me this stopover. Now let's get out of this most unpromising place as quickly as we can."

It was not possible to book an extra first class seat on the Chicago to Denver flight, so it was arranged that Kamala would sit next to the Guru. He watched her intently as she arranged her things in the overhead bin and then sat down. Her neck and arms were smoothly tanned, and she looked to him altogether supple and strong and desirable.

"Do I tell you enough how perfectly lovely you are?"

Kamala met the Guru's eyes and placed a cool palm on his forehead then his cheek.

"You do."

From his window seat, the Guru saw that a rangy young man, stalled in the aisle, was eyeing Kamala with clear interest. The Guru noted the pronounced jaw and hollowed cheek. He wore a burgundy sweatshirt on which COLORADO was printed over a crest. He was handsome in the youthful fashion of the day. There was pronounced stubble along his cheek, and his tousled hair glistened with some kind of gel. He looked ahead down the aisle then, the Guru thought, down at Kamala's breasts.

The Guru leaned across the tray separating the seats.

"Excuse me," the Guru said loudly, "Would that be the University?" He pointed at the young man's chest.

"Excuse me?" The young man drew back uncertainly. The Guru detected a trace of fear, even disgust, in his eyes.

"Is that the University, at Boulder?"

The young man saw that it was possible to move on. "Yessir. U.C., Boulder."

When the young man had passed, the Guru said to Kamala, "They say it is a playground."

"Maybe it is a happy playground."

The Guru smiled and closed his eyes. He formed a clear image of the Northern Illinois University sweatshirt he had purchased at the university bookstore the afternoon of his arrival. It was dark blue, almost black, and the creamy white letters made an oval around the university seal. It had felt right, hung right. In the mirror he saw that it showed just the right amount of the collar of his white shirt.

18

The Arrival of the Owl

"You must be getting excited," Granny Mueller had said from the back seat as they passed the barns and cornfields on the way to DeKalb. "You are going to be the Muellers' first college man."

The Guru glanced across the front seat to his father at the wheel. His father's face was set in a faint smile.

Alone later in his dorm room, the Guru looked out the window over his desk and saw through the breaks in the leafy branches the other arrivals and their families streaming along the dappled walks. It was brightly, exactly as he had pictured it. He felt in the movement below a stirring, a profound opening up. When his books and blotter were in place, he affixed the borders of his schedule to the desktop with Scotch tape. He withdrew the bound ledger he would use as his Journal from the desk drawer and inscribed his name, address, and telephone number in the corner of the inside cover. The creamy ruled first page felt substantial, important beneath the pads of his fingertips. In careful block capitals the Guru inscribed

QUIET—PATIENCE—PERFECT KINDNESS

Danny Katz, his roommate from Highland Park, greeted him with a torrent of talk: bits of identifying detail, jokey observations, questions posed in such rapid succession they were impossible to answer. "You like a little music? I hope you like a little music. We got—we got...a little Elvis, a little Johnny Ray, a little Diamonds, a little DelVikings. You know? 'Dom dom dom dom *dah*, dom bee doo bee?' You know 'Come Go With Me'? Hey it's O.K. if you don't. You don't like my stuff, I'll play it when you're out. Hey, I'm easy to live with. So where abouts is Palatine? That down state somewhere? You a smoker? I'm kind of a smoker, but if it bothers you, I'll do it when you're out. Am I easy to live with or what? Have some guys been up looking for me? I told some guys I know from home to stop up. Anybody come by? A guy named Kaplan? A really tall beanpole of a guy? Maybe they're in the Union. You checked out the Union? Interested in checking out the Union?"

In time the Guru came to like Danny Katz's presence and to find his banter benignly atmospheric. Danny Katz added an undemanding liveliness to the dorm room. He made the Guru welcome among his Highland Park friends in the Dining Hall and in the Union, and he did not seem to mind if the Guru declined and stayed behind. The Guru found the solitary silences richer for following Danny Katz's incessant talk.

It was Danny Katz who had labeled him Owl.

The Guru had been reviewing his Comparative Religion notes at his desk; and Danny Katz and his friend Dickstein were lounging on the bunk, trading banter, making plans for Homecoming Weekend.

"Jesus, Katz," Dickstein was saying. "How long do you think you could go on talking without stopping for air? How'd you get such a jet-propelled mouth? *Mueller*, how can you live with this guy? How can you stand it?"

The Guru smiled into his notes.

"Mueller," Danny Katz said, "unlike you, Dickstein, dick head, knows how to listen, how to carry on a decent conversation."

"How would you know? Have you ever let him say anything?"

"Harris," Danny Katz called across the room. "Harris, tell this ignoramus what a good conversationalist I am, what good conversations we have."

The Guru considered a response.

"I notice," Dickstein said, "he's not racing to agree with you."

"No," Danny Katz said. "Because, unlike you, mister motor mouth yourself, Mueller actually takes in what a person says. He listens for the deep wisdom, the *meat*, in what a person like me has to say."

"You'd have to listen for about twelve years to get the meat of what you have to say," said Dickstein.

"I can do that," the Guru said.

For a moment no one spoke. Then Danny Katz said, "My point exactly. I rest my case."

"Your case of shit."

"There you go with your gutter talk, Dickstein. Can't make his point, so he goes to 'your case of shit.' Harris, should we ask this guy to leave? He's bringing down the tone. See, when it's just Harris and me, we talk. We talk about the big issues of life. *Because*—Harris listens. Back in Palatine, he learned to listen."

"How do you know he's listening? How do you know he's not bored shitless?"

"No, that's just you, Dickstein. Did you know only bores are bored? A very great man, a famous man, said that. Now Harris listens to me and he is not bored. He takes it in, takes it all in, and then—"

"Then what?" Dickstein said.

"And then he says something extremely intelligent back, something he has really thought about. Harris is like a—like a wise owl. Aren't you, Harris? Look at him."

The Guru looked up from his notes.

"You're an owl. An owl *exactly*. Harris, you're the owl of Northern Illinois."

19

Christ and Buddha

Dr. Demas had taken a special interest in the Guru's assigned paper on Christ and Buddha. His neatly inked comments filled up most of the title page.

> *This is very interesting work. The minus after the* $\underline{A}$ *does not signify any slight withholding of approval or praise; rather, it is a little acknowledgement that your paper departed decisively from the guidelines I set down in the assignment. My feeling has always been that if a student ignores the parameters of an assignment and takes off on his own—it better be good! I must say I was interested in every word you wrote. You strike a prophetic, oracular tone, and you do well with it. While you do not ground your many declarations in the assigned readings, they seem to me congruent with the sacred texts. Again, your oracular tone rings true. I was especially taken by your conclusion. See comments inside.* $\underline{A\text{-}}$.

The Guru turned at once to the last page of the paper.

> *It would be simply false, then, to conclude that there is Christ "and" Buddha. Christ and Buddha were not in the world as two*

distinct persons at different points in time. Christ and Buddha are not like Washington and Lincoln. Only in a merely material world are Christ and Buddha separate "events." If Christ and Buddha are separate and different, then Buddha's Samsara and Christ's Nazareth are "the real world." But they are not the real world, for if they are the real world, then Christ and Buddha are not real. Or they are real only as Washington and Lincoln are real. The eternal, transcendent truth and mystery of Christ and Buddha is that their Reality registered in the material, historical world but only in order to show that it is an illusion. The Reality of Christ and Buddha is the same Reality, Reality itself. Buddha is of course Christ, and Christ is of course Buddha. There was no "and." There is no "and."

The Guru discovered—felt drawn up into—the liberating authority of Of Course. The force of Of Course came to dominate first his university papers, then his conversation and argument. "Of course Time is important—if there is Time. But of course there is no Time. There is of course a convention of Time, which is why we are early or late. But one is never early or late for Reality. There is no early or late in Reality. In Reality we have always been there, and Reality has always been. What is early or late is of course consciousness. Consciousness is held in a succession of Time Cages, until of course consciousness is able to embrace the illusion of the Time cage itself. That of course is a big step. This is why we have Masters. This is why we need God-men."

The Guru saw his University days as a dynamic unity. In all seasons he felt held in the same golden, burnished light, the light of crystalline autumn afternoons through the red and gold leaves beyond his window. From a great, sweet, quiet distance he came to treasure the haphazard dance of the others around him, streaming in and out of the lecture halls, the library, the Union. In the distance there was always a drum-pulse, the muted roar of a big Game.

Professor Demas helped him concentrate a special major in Comparative Religion and, in his sophomore year, encouraged him to revive the East-West Club. At the first session in the Student Seminar Room, only four students appeared: the towering and defeated looking Elsa Nygaard who wanted to be a missionary, Jacob Levy in his dark suit and yarmulke, tiny Ray Tsen, and the Guru. When it was clear no one else would appear, they introduced themselves, and the Guru asked, "Where should we start?" At first no one spoke. Then Ray Tsen, his squirrel face seemingly captive behind the lenses of his black plastic glasses, said, "Let's start we make special food."

Like the contours of an ancient rock face he was climbing, the great names in the history of religion, the renowned translators and editors of the sacred texts, the saints and heroes of Christian theology became known to the Guru. In time the library's theology collection, the journals and quarterlies in the Reference Room, grew finite, became a comfort. Between the foot of his bed and the closet he assembled a book case of pine boards and bricks, and to his Bible and assigned texts, he began adding his own selections: *A Treasury of the World's Religious Thought*, *Christ and Caesar* by Will and Ariel Durant, *What is a Yogi?* By Steve Karas, *The Bhagarad-Gita*, *Siddhartha* by Hermann Hesse, *The Prophet* by Kahlil Gibran, *The Way of Zen* by Alan Watts.

On a weekend excursion with the East-West Club to Chicago, he had spent a pleasing afternoon in the Philosophy and Religion department of Kroch's and Brentano's bookstore on Michigan Avenue. Every page of every book seemed a delicious invitation to read on. At length, having little money to spend, he purchased a miniature volume, bound in glossy yellow, of Zen koans.

One night, late, the Guru was reading in bed, rapt in the koans. Danny Katz entered the room, shattering the silence. He pulled the Guru's chair away from his desk and sat down hard.

"Oh, man," he said. "Am I shit faced."

The Guru met his eyes.

"So what's that you're reading?"

The Guru told him it was a collection of Zen koans and that koans were like puzzles which, when you thought about them, opened up your mind.

"Hey, I know some Cohns. I know Sammy Cohn, Josh Cohn, and Rabbi Lester Cohn, but I don't know any Zen Cohns."

The Guru laughed. "No, I don't think you do."

"Owl, tell me a Zen Cohn," Danny Katz said, closing his eyes and slumping in the chair.

The Guru read Danny Katz a koan about a monk who as a young man was told by his master to speak only if what he had to say was kind and true and necessary. Attempting to keep this standard, the monk never spoke again and achieved Enlightenment.

"So that's a Zen Cohn," Danny Katz said. "Huhh. Doesn't look like Enlightenment for me, Harris. Do you think?"

"Do you want to be Enlightened?"

"Yeah. *Shit*, yeah."

"Well then you're on your way."

Danny Katz undressed and went down the hall to the bathroom. The Guru switched off the reading lamp and lay back. He felt warmly—he felt love—for Danny Katz. *I am home.* The Guru concentrated so that he would remember to enter the words, *I am home*, into his journal in the morning.

20
The Guru Arises

In his senior year the Guru arranged to share an apartment with another Religion major, Eliott Bourne. The apartment was a partitioned warren of rooms on the third floor of an old frame house on the outskirts of DeKalb. Waking on his mattress tucked under the eaves to the Sunday morning quiet or reading in the lumpy upholstered chair in the little living room, inhaling the heavy sweetness of Eliott Bourne's pipe smoke, the Guru felt as if he had already finished his university life. He felt agreeably lethargic and old.

Eliott Bourne was a dramatic presence in the Religion Department, and he was a dramatic presence in the apartment. He had transferred from the University of Chicago when, as he said, he ran out of money. When the Guru asked him about Chicago, Eliott Bourne had said: "It's a real university, maybe the best in the world." Eliott Bourne spoke of Northern Illinois with contempt. "It's somewhere," he said, "between the army and four more years of high school." Eliott Bourne had not attended high school; he had attended the Wells School, a boarding school in Connecticut. He had lived a year in London. He had spent summers backpacking through Europe. For months after leaving Chicago he had traveled in India. His unruly brown hair flew back like wings from a center part, and he wore, seemingly always, an elaborately stitched fisherman's sweater over shapeless and worn corduroys. Eliott Bourne was twenty-five.

One night the Guru heard through the thin wall next to his head Eliott Bourne and his girl friend talking about him from their bed. The Guru heard the girl friend make a muffled reference to his name. "What do you mean," Eliott Bourne had said. "He's the absolute perfect roommate. All he does is read and study. He buys food. He cleans up. He keeps out of the way. He makes no noise. He's perfect."

Eliott Bourne smoked marijuana. He had first tried marijuana when he was traveling with friends in North Africa. At Chicago he had made friends with other marijuana users. In India, he told the Guru, marijuana was incredibly cheap.

"Is it used for sacred purposes?" The Guru had asked.

"Not that I could tell," Eliott Bourne said.

"In ancient India marijuana was used by Hindus as a sacrament to achieve transcendence. Later yoga was adopted instead, and it is said to carry you farther."

"Have you ever blown pot, Owl?"

"No, I haven't."

"Any time you want to try."

"Thank you."

The Guru thought smoking marijuana furtively in Eliott Bourne's pipe would be sordid. He imagined it spreading like a brown stain, weighing down his Clarity. Thinking about it made him tired.

In May of that year, the sunny, slow week between the successful completion of his exams and Commencement, the Guru eyed Eliott Bourne's pipe on the mantle. It lay on its side next to the old-fashioned china saltshaker in which Eliott Bourne kept his wadded stash of marijuana. Eliott would be out finishing his exams all day. The Guru had nothing scheduled to do.

His heart quickened as he sat down in the upholstered chair. He pressed the flakes and seeds of the marijuana down into the bowl of the pipe with his finger, then lit a match over the bowl and drew hard on the pipe stem. There was a kind of hissing and bubbling in the bowl, and the Guru could feel the acrid smoke passing harshly over his tongue and down into his throat. The smoke chafed and burned impossibly as he tried to hold it in his lungs, and he coughed painfully. He lit the pipe and inhaled a half dozen more times, then looked down into the bowl of the pipe and saw what looked like spent ash. The Guru put the pipe aside, lay his head back in the chair and closed his eyes. He felt agitated, his heart still beating quickly. He breathed slowly and deeply to calm himself. His mouth was coated and sour from the smoke, and his throat felt charred and raw. In a few minutes the agitation abated, and his head felt clear. He decided to get up, move about the apartment. He returned Eliott Bourne's pipe to its place on the mantle. With mild disappointment, but also with relief, the Guru was aware that he was unaltered; nothing had happened.

The Guru read for a while in the upholstered chair. The day had grown warm, and he dropped off to sleep. When he awoke, the burnt, coated feeling on his tongue reminded him that he had smoked marijuana. Without deliberation, he arose, refilled the bowl of the pipe, tamping down the old ashes, and sat down to try again. Again, he was able to manage six or seven searing inhalations before his throat was stinging unpleasantly. The pipe bowl, when he looked, showed only grey ash.

Again the Guru lay his head back and closed his eyes. The agitation would not this time disperse; he felt a clenching in his chest, his heart held in a shallow current. Then it was as if the base of his skull was vibrating with the current, and he knew that he was going to erupt with it, and then he did. There was a static roar, the achievement of something like a great toneless chord, and then his awareness swelled out beyond and above his head. He experienced himself as a shimmering bubble containing his body as he sat, and his wonder and pleasure in this gave way to an overwhelming eruption of a still greater pleasure, and then there was a close succession of such eruptions, as the bubble reformed in concentric rings. The Guru was aware of the tingling in his feet, in his hands, in seemingly every cell. A mild breeze suspended a flap of gauzy curtain almost horizontally out over the windowsill before drifting back to rest. But the Guru realized he had not done this. He realized he had not yet breathed.

That afternoon the Guru walked by himself into DeKalb and made his way without deliberation to the stadium. He passed through an unlocked gate and climbed midway up into the empty stands. Down below a crew was removing wooden folding chairs from the back of a truck for Commencement. The Guru heard and didn't hear the rhythmic slap of wood on wood.

That night the Guru wrote in his Journal: "And of course if anyone whatsoever requires Proof, that person needs only to smoke marijuana, remembering that to prove Reality is not to possess it."

III

The Guru Shares

1

To Starshower

Kamala tapped his shoulder, and the Guru opened his eyes.

"We're about to land," she said.

"Yes."

Between his heart and the great mound of his belly the Guru felt a beckoning heaviness and warmth, as if he were being drawn back down into sleep. He blinked his eyes. For a moment he could not imagine rising from the seat, standing up in the aisle, walking.

"It has been such a long time." The Guru smiled, closing his eyes.

"Since a Sharing, yes," said Kamala.

"Absolutely right."

"Sorry?"

"The Sharings will be absolutely right," the Guru said. "They will be magnificent."

As the Entourage waited in the President's Club for the driver who would take them from the airport to Starshower Cascade, Andy-dam was able to access updated developments on the Sharings from his laptop.

"Things are moving quickly," he reported to the others. "We have two hundred and twenty now, and we should probably close off registrants by noon tomorrow. We could easily be at capacity. Phyllis said the phones have not stopped ringing since we posted."

"So we will have them by tomorrow evening, and Sunday we can begin," said the Guru.

"Yes," said Andy-dam. We can assemble at six for a Greeting, then provide a light meal."

"Exactly right," said the Guru.

"Oh, and guess what else?" Andy-dam said. "Gannett Witherspoon is signed up. Gannett's coming. Apparently he was one of the first to call."

2
Gannett Witherspoon

Gannett Witherspoon had been one of The Nine, indeed, along with Andy and Trish Triester, a driving force when they were moving past Heartsorrow and into the Movement. It was Gannett who, as publicist and chronicler of the early years, first called them The Nine. As a young associate professor of religious studies at S.U.N.Y. Buffalo, he had come to Santa Barbara to collect data for his first book, *Cults and Community in the Age of Aquarius*. There he made the Guru's acquaintance at the Rama Krishna Meditation Center. In the course of interviewing youthful devotees to Hare Krishna, The Maharishi, Kerpal Singh, and the Church of Scientology, Gannett Witherspoon was struck by occasional references to an unaffiliated young mystic—"kind of a guru," someone had said, "An American guy"—who had set up on his own in the Meditation Center Reading Room. Gannett Witherspoon had wanted to meet him. "Ask for the Owl," he was told.

The morning Gannett Witherspoon finally spotted him, The Guru was propped up on an arrangement of cushions on the floor at a corner of the Reading Room. Andy Horvitz and Trish Triester were sitting cross-legged at his feet as were another young man and woman who, Gannet thought when he could see their faces, looked drugged or ill. Andy Horvitz's eyes were fixed on the floor in front of him, and the Guru was barking with what seemed to Gannett Witherspoon unnatural laughter.

"Do you see why?" the Guru prodded. "Do you see why I have to laugh at you?"

"I am trying to see," Andy said quietly. "Could you help me to see?"

The Guru threw back his head and let out a loud sharp "hah!" He said to Andy, "Help you to *see*? You can see if you choose to, if you really want to. You have a mind. You have eyes."

The Guru looked up to acknowledge Gannett Witherspoon.

"Welcome. Come join us. I am just in the process of helping my friend Andy here to stop being pitiful." The Guru leaned forward and rapped his knuckles on the floor in front of Andy. "To stop being *pitiful*," he repeated loudly. "And laughable and *a*sinine and slavish and humble pie and fake, fake holy and pious. That's what we're doing, aren't we, Andy?"

"Yes. We are," said Andy.

"And we love you," said Trish Triester leaning her forehead into the shoulder of Andy's tee shirt. "I love you. Everybody loves you."

"That's right," said the Guru. "We love you too much to let you play humble-mumble inside your pitiful ego, your pitiful desperate ego. Do you hear me, Andy? Really hear me? Love will not let you play humble Andy. Love wants Real Andy. You know that your humility is a fraud. Your humility is not humble. It isn't real. It's pride, Andy. It's all ego."

Andy sat in silence, his eyes still downcast.

"So why not drop it?" The Guru made a tossing gesture. "Throw it away."

"How?" Andy asked.

"*How?* You know what to do with bullshit. First, you have to admit it's bullshit. So start there. Start by saying 'my humility is bullshit'."

"My humility is bullshit."

"Good. And now say, 'having to be told it's bullshit is bullshit.'"

"And having to be told it's bullshit is bullshit."

"Good. And now say 'and agreeing to everything like a submissive wimp is bullshit'."

"And submitting to everything like a submissive wimp is bullshit."

"Good. Because submitting to bullshit is bullshit."

"Submitting to bullshit is bullshit."

"And this is bullshit."

"And this is bullshit."

The Guru broke into laughter, infectious falsetto screams of laughter. Trish Triester was laughing. The drugged couple was laughing. The Guru looked up at Gannett Witherspoon, who was still standing at a distance. Gannett Witherspoon too had begun to laugh.

"*Such* bullshit," the Guru shouted happily.

Andy Horvitz looked up. He broke into a smile, and the smile ignited more laughter, and Andy Horvitz was laughing.

"And here at last," sang out the Guru, "is Andy! Thank God for the Real Andy—and for my incredible bullshit!"

Gannett Witherspoon spent the weeks following his initial meeting with the Guru listening to him teach in the Reading Room, interviewing those who came casually or regularly to hear him. When, occasionally, he found the Guru alone, he would ask questions and record the answers into his battery operated tape recorder.

"So I will be in your book?" The Guru said. Gannett Witherspoon thought he looked amused.

"Yes, I think you will."

"Do you think your book will transform the world?"

Gannet Witherspoon looked hard into the Guru's eyes. He wanted to know if he was being put on.

"I don't know about that," he said cautiously.

"If I wrote a book," the Guru said, "I would want it to transform the world."

"Have you ever thought about writing one?"

"It is not necessary."

For a moment neither of them spoke, then Gannett Witherspoon said, "It's not necessary to transform the world?"

"You see, for me"—the Guru's tone was warm, intimate—"the world is already transformed, already perfect. It has always been perfect, and this *maya* we stumble through is egotism and confusion."

A grant of thirty-five thousand dollars from the National Endowment for the Humanities enabled Gannett Witherspoon to take a full year's leave from the university and to finish *Cult and Community* in Santa Barbara. The long chapter on the Guru and his work, "From Owl to Yogananda Avatar," became the centerpiece of the finished study and won the book considerable attention, as well as many new followers for the Guru. The stream of pilgrim visitors often filled the Reading Room beyond capacity, so that listeners would be poised attentively in the doorways and far down the hallway in either direction.

Because the Guru was technically only a visitor to the Rama Krishna Center and a user of its library and Reading Room, it was soon felt that he should assemble his followers in his own quarters. Andy Horvitz, re-christened Andy-dam Beloved Disciple, looked after the arrangements for relocating their sessions, first at the Y.M.C.A., then in a lecture hall of the University's Continuing Education Center. Gannett Witherspoon himself had helped Andy-dam with these negotiations and had also been influential in identifying financial supporters including, ultimately, Curtis Forbes, an early devotee, one of The Nine, and a multi-millionaire.

Not long after the successful publication of *Cult and Community*, critics began to question Gannett Witherspoon's objectivity. There seemed, the critical voices said, to be no clear distinction between reporting and advocacy. Where the Guru and his work were concerned, it was claimed, Witherspoon had lost his critical perspective.

At first Gannett Witherspoon had taken pains to defend himself against these charges. He argued strongly for the objectivity and verifiability of everything he had reported about the Guru. But when he was asked, at a scholarly conference convened at University College, London, on "The New Faces of Fundamental-ism," whether he thought the Guru was "another California fad" or, possibly, a genuine western instance of a yogic presence, Gannett Witherspoon heard himself, as if from some other place in the hall, respond: "I just have to say, after sitting with the guy for over a year, I think he's the real thing."

That year Gannett Witherspoon gave up tenure at the Univer-sity and accepted Adjunct status in order to oversee publications and other communications for what the Guru and The Nine were now calling The Movement.

The years following were the most turbulent and disturb-ing—and certainly the most vivid—of his life. With the excep-tion of the Guru himself, none of the earlier followers, certainly none of The Nine, had prepared for the velocity at which the Guru became first nationally and then internationally known. Skeptics and debunkers linked the emergent Movement with Pop Culture tendencies to look eastward and inward. The Beatles and other celebrities had taken up with self-styled gurus. Booksellers could not keep Herman Hesse's novels and Alan Watts' Zen commen-taries in stock. Yoga and Transcendental Meditation classes were heavily subscribed in the great urban hubs and in the quietest towns and villages.

After the Viet Nam War, when the youthful sense of urgency and new possibility began to abate, the Movement experienced its first direct challenge, what Gannett Witherspoon would chronicle later as "The *New Mind* Wars."

Stimulated at least in part by the wide distributions of the first two books of his teachings, *The Mystery of Pleasure,* and the *Ecstasy of the Cells*, the Guru's celebrity began to evoke something close to hysteria in his new followers. Extravagant claims were made by cross-country pilgrims who claimed to experience *darshon* even while approaching Santa Barbara on the freeway. Audiences and the designated Sharers who were granted more intimate exchanges emerged ecstatic, often, in Gannett Witherspoon's phrase, "incoherent with bliss" after having heard, touched, or even caught a glimpse of the Guru.

While the *New Mind's* editorial campaign to debunk him would finally succeed in raising doubts, several earlier journalistic attempts to locate and candidly report on the man "behind" the mystic's façade had turned into respectful and even appreciative witnesses to the Guru's transformative effect. "Until," a reporter for the *Los Angeles Times Magazine* wrote, "I attended, tongue solidly lodged in cheek, a pre-Sharing of a self-styled Yogi from Illinois now billed as Yogananada Avatar, I had thought 'wept for joy' was a figure of speech." Even before the Guru appeared on the elevated platform, the audience surrounding the reporter had bobbed their heads spastically in anticipatory *kriyas*. There was some delicate flute music, he reported, followed by a single sustained droning note, as if from a bagpipe. And then, seemingly without arriving, the Guru appeared. "And in an instant all were on their feet, arms raised high. The men and women to my left and right were weeping, some silently, some convulsively. I turned around and realized that everyone was weeping. Then—and I want to but cannot say 'to my astonishment'—I felt my own eyes well up with tears and my throat constrict painfully. I held my pad in one hand, a pen in the other, and all I could think was: the only thing possible now is to surrender to this."

Some conservative Catholic journals with modest circulations published review essays of Gannett Witherspoon's book and of his subsequent editions of the Guru's teachings. The Catholic essays were sharp, closely reasoned, and finally dismissive. The Catholic writers found the Guru "airy and cryptic," "ultimately pantheistic," "both ethically and spiritually inert." One critic found the Guru's teaching agreeable enough, but offering nothing not already maintained by a convinced Christian.

The Catholics' objections appeared at the feverish height of the Guru's celebrity and made no detectable impact. Gannett Witherspoon was fascinated, however, to read in some of the Sharers' exit questionnaires, that they had *come to* the Guru's teachings after having read the critical articles. The Guru himself beamed with pleasure when he heard this. On the spot Gannet Witherspoon determined that he would contact those Catholic Sharers who had signed their questionnaires to learn exactly what had so stimulated their interest.

"Yes!" The Guru had agreed. "In the true flow of things, negativity itself depolarizes and is swept into the positive. It can happen. It happens."

Documenting this process later in *The New Mind Wars*, Gannett Witherspoon, still sensitive to being dismissed as a publicist for the Movement, took pains to cite the most vigorous *New Mind* criticisms of the Guru's teaching:

> . . . *The self-styled guru now calling himself Yaganandu Avatar was up until a year or so ago a nonpaying hanger-on at the Rama Krishan Meditation Center in Santa Barbara. He registered for Reading Room privileges there under the name Harris Mueller. As Harris Mueller, he is recorded as having earned a B.A. in Religious Studies from Northern Illinois University. At the Meditation Center he was known to engage strangers in not always welcome conversation. Nevertheless, a small following emerged who were fond of quoting Mueller's gnomic utterances, since expanded at great length in pamphlets and now books.*

> *Not long after he became a regular in the Reading Room, he shed the name Harris Mueller in favor of The Owl. There is something undeniably owlish in his countenance. Small features are clustered at the center of a large, round, fleshy face. Continuous eyebrows make a sheltering arc over an already disconcerting stare.*

> *The Owl is given to long monologues. His language tends to abstraction, and there is much repetition. One early listener likened his talk to that of an undergraduate impersonating a professor. There*

is a great deal of "And so you see" and "one must conclude" and (with numbing frequency) "of course." His themes, if that is the right word, are that time is an illusion and that the world and everyone in it are already perfect, although the latter, due to an illusion of their self-importance, fail to recognize their deeper condition and are thus unhappy. No harm in this, of course, except that the Buddha, Christ, and even Mary Baker Eddy have covered this ground more compellingly and certainly more eloquently—than has Harris Mueller/Owl/Yogananda Avatar...

--"Just in from the Midwest," New Mind

Rather than take issue with specific points and biases in the *New Mind* articles, Gannett Witherspoon simply alternated passages of the criticisms with selected teachings from the Guru's books.

The plague of our era is negativity. Men, women, and children everywhere are contracted, armored, bitter with negativity. The very language of learning is shot through with analysis, dissection, doubt and dread. In this era, we are disillusioned before we can even be illusioned! We flee, we fall sickeningly to the pole of negativity. We lionize the supreme doubter, the ultimate critic. The final, unarticulated dream of negativity is to see through—everything. For what? In order to what? The negativists never ask. They do not ask because the answer is to them devastating. It is so that they can maintain their anxious illusion of control. I doubt therefore I am. I debunk therefore I matter. But of course each of us already and forever matters. We matter so perfectly and completely that we need not give a thought to "mattering." This, however, is a terrifying prospect for the terrified negativist.

--From The Mystery of Pleasure

. . .What are we afraid of? Why are people even afraid of me? To put it simply, we are afraid because something small and desperate, something other fearful people have taught us, is fighting to hold ecstasy at bay. There is a rampant, unarticulated rumor. The rumor says: be on guard for ecstasy. Close your eyes to it. Clench your teeth against it. By all means don't open up to it sexually! Don't let it in! Don't let it out! Hang on! Contract! Don't lose yourself! Don't surrender!

But you can. You must. In the deepest way you already have. Undress. Go naked into the sunshine. Raise your arms, raise your voice. You can give up to it and give it up. You can go home. You are already home.

--From The Ecstasy of the Cells

. . .Perhaps you have seen what they are saying about me. That I am a delusional leader of a Cult. That, like Rasputin, I am bending helpless followers to my will. They sound as if they are afraid of me. What exactly are they afraid of? Can you imagine being afraid of me? Can you imagine being afraid of my body, my physical force? Could you imagine being mesmerized or hypnotized by me? Going out and committing some violent or ruinous act on my account? Could I initiate you into an organization? Force you to join something? Compel

you to march? Have I asked you for money? Could I make you give me money?

If not, what are they afraid of? Could it be because I am happy? Could it be because you are happy? Could it be because we have been seen to be carried in the current of ecstasy?

--from "We Are Not a Cult"

3

The Defection of Trish Triester

Whether or not *New Mind* articles dubious about the Guru's teaching took any appreciable toll on his early following, the long interview with Trish Triester published in *New Mind* after she left the Movement caused a considerable stir.

Not long after their initial encounter in Santa Barbara, Trish Triester became a *kanya*, or Heart Consort, of the Guru—his first. As she confessed candidly in the interview, she did not then know anything about the yogic status of a *kanya* in the Asian tradition, nor really did she care. "I was just blissfully happy in the presence of my new teacher. This is when everyone called him the Owl. It is hard to describe the feeling. It's like melting or thawing. All the defenses go down and you want to just open up to it, open your arms, your whole self to it—and so (*beaming smile, laughter*) I did.

"Sleeping with him, sex, felt like the most natural thing in the world. It was like...the physical completion of what had already happened when I met him. What can I say? It was like my cells were alive and buzzing with this new positivity, and I could feel myself just kind of dissolving into him, swimming into him. Everybody felt it. Sex was just a way to express it, the sexual way. It didn't feel daring or forbidden at all. There was no pressure, no special ego in it—like, 'now I'm the special one'—I was just suspended in that feeling in a new way."

Occasionally, in the early years, new followers were confused or apprehensive that the Guru had sexual relations with certain devotees. The Guru's *kanyas* were not casual favorites, nor were they committed partners. "Where sexual love is concerned," the Guru had written in *The Ecstasy of the Cells*, "the western mind is comforted by categories and restrictions, especially where holy men are involved. Westerners are relieved by Celibacy. They can live with Wife. But the fluid, ecstatic, sexual communion of soul and soul is too great, too thrilling for the contracted ego to grasp."

For several years there were four more or less established *kanyas.* Then after the All-the World Sharing in Maui, the number grew to six, then expanded briefly to eleven. Initiates and even Life Sharers could no longer say with confidence who was a *kanya* and who was not. The exception of course was Trish Triester who, because she had been the first, and one of the Nine, seemed somehow to hold a special place in the Movement. Unlike the later *kanyas*, Trish Triester would never bear a child by the Guru, nor, like them, would she assume a quiet, anonymous role among the Sharers.

Trish Triester, the Guru himself had exclaimed with pleasure, "was a *presence!*" She was a big woman. Her long center-parted hair was honey-gold, and it framed a strong, animated face. A ruddy healthiness glowed through her fair skin. Her body, on the verge of plumpness, created a pleasing sense of both ripeness and availability. Her bright *saris* fell luxuriously over ample, unfettered breasts and down along her rounded hips. She struck almost everyone who met her as excitingly beautiful even when, recalled afterwards, specific features did not seem to account for her stunning effect. She was also undeniably photogenic. The Movement's early printed publications and videos featured many candid, rapt images of Trish Triester among the Sharers.

The *New Mind* reporter was of course interested in the sexual particulars of her experience as a *kanya* and, above all, in the reasons for her leaving The Movement. About the former, she was not finally very disclosing, despite her earthy candor otherwise. "It doesn't make any sense to talk about specific sex—sex acts—with Him," she told the interviewer. "It's just that when you were with Him, usually alone but not always, and you felt yourself held in that wonderful overwhelming *frequency*, you just *did* it, gave yourself up to it. You know? It was wonderful, but how can I say it—*light?* It was like playing, in a lovely way."

Trish Triester left the Movement, she said, because, she couldn't feel "the magic" any more. "It got big," she said, "and the whole thing seemed to be driven by organizational business and planning. There were meetings, meetings first thing in the morning, sometimes meetings all day long. She acknowledged that Sharings were almost always beautiful, but there was, she said, "A grindiness to it. There was so much travel and deadlines and tension. Then He started to get sick. We'd hear about it and then He'd just be gone—disappear—and then the whole thing for us started to get crazy."

"I got out," Trisha Triester concluded, "but I'm not going to knock it. He opened me up, changed me forever. I think a lot of people are still finding that, and that's good. But something just told me I have that now, I did that, I don't have to keep doing it. I'm looking forward to sitting still, in one place. Actually, I'm on *fire* to do that."

Gannet Witherspoon would learn later that the editors of *New Mind* almost declined to run the interview. Despite revelations of the technically polygamous arrangement of the Guru and his Kanyas, the disclosures from Trish Triester fell far short of the sensational, seamy revelations the editors had anticipated. In the end, the decision to print the piece was swayed by the allure of the proposed photographs. They showed Trisha and other Kanyas in attitudes of transported worship. There were some shots of the Kanyas holding the Guru's babies. There was a striking picture of Trish Triester emerging half naked from the surf. Each woman depicted was eye-catching and decidedly sexy, and the locations—the Rockies, the Caribbean, Pacific Islands—were lush and brilliantly sunlit.

Gannett Witherspoon also suggested that Trish Triester's paid advance for the interview, five thousand dollars, was no small consideration in the editors' decision to publish.

4

Astral Pain

For months the letters column of *New Mind* was given over almost entirely to spirited exchanges between detractors and supporters of the Guru. The sum effect of the controversy, Gannett Witherspoon would conclude, was that it enhanced the Guru's public profile and brought new seekers to the Movement.

The Movement received a far more powerful boost when it was revealed that the members of the eclectic and wildly popular band, Astral Pain, had become devotees. Over a period of several weeks, seemingly every newspaper tabloid and celebrity magazine featured stories and pictures of the charismatic, emaciated-looking face of Woody Woodman, the band's lead singer and rhythm guitar player, confirming his and his band-mates' adherence to the Guru's teachings. Perhaps without knowing it, Woodman may also have helped to put the *New Mind* and other attacks in a clearer perspective.

"The critics and intellectuals all miss the point," he told a reporter from *Rolling Stone*. "This isn't about which big theory is right or wrong or if the guy's got the right credentials. That's not even the right game. This is about opening up, freeing yourself from —from small stuff we think is big stuff. The Teacher's message is that we can have it all, have the real thing. We already have it. We just have to shed our shit. There's no *debate* about this. This is about the *heart*, not the head."

There followed a relatively quiet period during which Woodman and the other members of Astral Pain stopped commenting to the press. For nearly a year the band did not tour or record. They were observed in attendance at a series of Sharings at Star Shower, but they were not, as some observers had speculated, "featured" as entertainers. Other attendees noted that Astral Pain did seem to enjoy a privileged relationship to the Guru. There were reports of special *darshons* and direct teachings, of evening meals taken with the Guru, even socializing into the small hours. Initiates from the Santa Barbara days remembered the Guru's enthusiasm for Astral Pain's early recordings.

From Star Shower, a short, formal press release was issued to the effect that the band members had embarked, like thousands of others, on a program of spiritual teaching conducted by the Master Yogananda Avatar. The master was reported to find the Astral Pain members "honest and dedicated, delightful friends."

Because Woody Woodman and Astral Pain's drummer, Farr Rockaway, were notorious for abusing alcohol and drugs, the rock press began raising the question of whether the band's new spirituality would also entail their sobriety. And if so, what effect would it have on their subsequent music, on their androgynous, bad-boy stage personae? Or, ran another line of rumor and speculation, did the band party *with* the Guru who, it was noted, had never opined negatively on psychoactive drugs or about the limits of sensual experiences of any kind? Years later, Woodman confided to a biographer that his time with the Movement had indeed been a breakthrough for him spiritually. "In a way," he said, "We were on top of the world. Our concerts were all sold out. Our records were huge. But I was sleepwalking through all that, usually stoned out of my mind. I remember when we first started reading the Teachings and after I met Him, thinking, *good*, this is going to be quiet and safe for a while. It's going to be clear. Someone good is in charge." About His drug use then and the rumors of the band's getting high with the Guru, Woodman said, "That whole idea is so beside the point. He didn't need to get high. "Man, He was already there. I never saw anything change Him, mushrooms, acid—anything."

Then, after nearly a year of musical silence from Astral Pain, they released *Hymns to Yogananda*. As many critics noted, their strategy, from a marketing standpoint, was brilliant. By virtually disappearing from the public while their popularity was sharply ascending, the combined curiosity and impatience on the part of their fans had reached a nearly crazed pitch by the time *Hymns to Yogananda* appeared. As one reviewer wrote, "Even their silence seemed to work on us, to the extent that, truth to tell, we would have stormed the mall for *anything* they put out."

Nearly all listeners found *Hymns to Yogananda* baffling. Except for the band's familiar acoustic guitars and their trademark treble harmonies, there was little musical continuity with their previous work.

On first hearing, especially, the various cuts were hard to distinguish from one another. Against the insistent repetitions of a single tonic chord, almost always G, stuck by guitar and sitar together, a series of vocal lines would meander upward, and when the dominant chord, D, was sounded, a single vocal line was repeated for the duration of the hymn. Some of the first reviewers found the sustained repetitions unendurably irritating. "I challenge anybody to listen to three of these 'hymns' consecutively without at least thinking about banging your head against the wall." Others were positive and receptive. The hymns should not be compared to earlier Astral Pain or to pop tunes at all, it was argued. They should be listened to as hymns, as prayers, as acts of worship. As such the "chant" quality of the recordings was appropriate. "Once past the realization that this is simply not the funky playfulness of the old Astral Pain," one critic wrote, "the hymns start to take hold of you. Go with them, and they become hypnotic."

Yogananda avatar

Comet trailing past my star

Eternity, nativity

Connect, connect, connect to me

Yo-ga-nan-da A-va-tar

Yo-ga-nan-da A-va-tar

Yo-ga-nan-da A-va-tar

Yo-ga-nan-da A-va-tar...

Despite the uncertain critical response to *Hymns to Yogananda*, the disc outsold by a vast margin anything Astral Pain had recorded previously. Sales mounted for months worldwide, causing some commentators to speculate that the recording was perhaps being acquired less for its musical appeal than for its value as a cultural artifact. "Having among one's souvenirs a plastic encased disc of *Hymns to Yogananda* may one day assume the value of previous generations' 3-d glasses, saddle shoes, or raccoon coats."

It is unlikely, however, that the impulse to preserve historic tokens could alone account for the phenomenal sales of *Hymns to Yananda*. The recording received as much radio play as might be due to a chart-topping hit, but air play alone could not explain why decades after the disc's release, lines of the verses and their refrains would rise so readily to the lips of both children and adults.

The sun is the light

And the light is the eye

And the eye opens bright

To the All of the sky

Yo-ga-nan-da O-pen me

Yo-ga-nan-da O-pen me

Yo-ga-nan-da O-pen me

Yo-ga-nan-da O-pen me...

To the Guru's devotees and the Star Shower Sharers, the hymns to the Master held another meaning altogether. For them, massed in the bracing meadow of the alpine compound, arm in arm, swaying together, heads whipped back in *kriya* rushes, the emergence into the cool blue air of Astral Pain's amplified hymns was not music *about* the Completeness of the Master's imminent presence; it simply *was* that presence, as music. On those transporting late afternoons, the rattling and hissing of the wind in the aspens served as a teasing prelude to the first amplified strain of the sitar, just as the hymns, taken up or mouthed in silence by the ecstatic Sharers, announced the bright presence of the Guru in their midst.

Astral Pain did not attempt another recording like *Hymns to Yogananda*. Until their dissolution, they achieved never less than moderate success with their tuneful, earthy reflections on love and loss and change. Their achievement of cult status, however, was finally inseparable from the impact of *Hymns*. More than one rock critic pointed out that a listener's immersion in *Hymns* somehow remade the context of the recordings that preceded it. "It is almost as if," one of them wrote, "to really lose yourself in the genius of Astral Pain, you have to first lose yourself in *Hymns to Yogananda*— and you have to do that on faith alone."

5

Oxycontin

Early brilliant sun whitened the Guru's sleeping suite. Andy-dam watched Kamala set down a tall glass of apple juice and remove the dish of uneaten slices of fruit and yogurt from the bedside table. When she was gone, he asked his question again.

"We are past our capacity for lodging and feeding the people who are arriving. We closed registration two full days ago, but they keep coming. The lots are full, the gates are closed, but they are backed up for miles along Route 9. They are walking up, leaving their cars. The state police want to know what to do. Should late arrivals be stopped at the gates? Should they be turned back?"

The Guru was sitting up in his bed, supported by a bank of white pillows. Andy-dam could not tell if he was listening to him. The Guru reached for the glass of apple juice and took a slow sip. He looked wonderfully at ease, rested and comfortable. He looked immovable.

"Are they peaceful?" The Guru asked. "Are they behaving themselves?"

"So far as I know. So far."

"Then let them come. We will feed them what we have." The Guru smiled broadly. "It will be like the fishes and the loaves."

"All our rooms are booked."

"The rooms must go to those who have registered. The rest must find their way back after the Sharing."

In the dark, Andy-dam thought to himself. He pictured the Sharers trying to make their way through the wooded paths, then down along the mountain road, in the dark.

"That must be the arrangement," the Guru said firmly.

Andy-dam felt an unexpected surge of confidence, of hope. "I'll go talk to the police."

As Andy-dam and Curtis Forbes rose to go, the Guru said, "Curtis, would you stay for a moment?"

Curtis drew his chair to the foot of the Guru's bed and sat down. The Guru looked alert, playful.

"Now, Curtis," the Guru said, "imagine my surprise when I was reading this morning's *Denver Post* and saw that there is a terrible new drug of abuse in the city. Do you know what it is?"

"No, I'm sorry," said Curtis Forbes, "I haven't seen the paper."

"It is"—the Guru leaned toward the bedside table and put down his glass of apple juice, picking up a plastic cylinder of prescription medicine—"it is called *oxycontin*, I believe." The Guru held up the cylinder of capsules and shook them. "My medicine! The prescription you have found for me."

The Guru widened his eyes and smiled questioningly at Curtis Forbes.

"Tell me about this dangerous drug."

"You're right," Curtis Forbes said. "The drug is an opiate. Taken in those capsules it's an excellent pain killer, but if you break them up into powder and take a lot of it, it can be a serious narcotic, like heroin."

"They are breaking into pharmacies to get it in Denver," the Guru said. "Killing the pharmacists."

Curtis Forbes smiled at the Guru, a slow, warm smile. "You haven't felt any such urges, have you?"

The Guru howled with laughter.

"Not yet! In fact, *mon docteur*, I woke up thinking what a thoroughly marvelous medicine it was, woke up feeling light as air, renewed, restored—then I read that I may be in the clutches of a terrible poison."

"It will not be a terrible poison if you use it as prescribed. But it is serious pain medication. If it troubles you at all, I can find something else."

"*By no means,*" the Guru said loudly, still in high spirits. "God forbid. In fact, make sure there is a good supply. The days ahead are going to be like nothing we have done before."

"And you are well?"

"I am, by the grace of God and *oxycontin,* the light of the world."

By nine o'clock the fruit and grains and juices were cleared from the breakfast tables in the Star Shower Refectory. The Sharers had begun to disperse out into the garden, the great meadow, and the alpine paths where they would do their Early Meditations. A morning *darshon* was scheduled at 10:30 for Return Sharers. The *darshon* would include a Direct Teaching from the Guru.

Andy-dam, striding briskly from the kiosk at the Main Gate, where he had been conferring with two officers from the State Highway patrol felt the radiant force of the autumn sunlight on his face and on his shoulders. The cool air tasted delicious and clean in his mouth, and he was all at once elated. The day was bright and fine, cloudless. The unexpected crowd would somehow amplify the bracing promise of the atmosphere. Approaching the main lodge, Andy-dam took in the purposeful files of colorfully robed Sharers as they spilled out over the green grounds of the compound.

Bathed now and lightly oiled, the Guru stood in his white silk trousers gazing out the window of his suite at the Sharers as they seated themselves in clusters dotting the great meadow. The sun made flashes of fire where it struck the sheen of their robes and shawls. The Guru imagined the force of the sunlight; let himself feel it on his upturned face. Behind him, Kamala had finished his braid and was offering an arm of a rose colored satin tunic. The tunic was accented with gold piping, and the buttons were disks of bright gold. Stepping around to look at him from the front, Kamala was pleased. He would not be rouged for the teaching *darshon*, but she noted with satisfaction that the fabric of the tunic cast a rosy wash over the massive planes of the Guru's face. She thought he looked flushed, at peace, glowing with health.

"Thank you, my love," the Guru said to Kamala. "I need to sit for a while by myself and prepare for my teaching."

Kamala exited the sleeping suite silently. The Guru moved to his night table and extracted his Teaching Journal from the drawer. He inclined himself comfortably against the pillows on his bed and opened the journal to his last entry:

Simplicity, Complexity

(only the particular)

Diamonds and Rhinestones

(The emptiness of authenticity)

The Guru felt the deep call to sleep which always preceded a teaching session. But, he realized again with pleasure, he felt good. There was no ache or special weight in his scrotum. He could feel no pain.

6
Simplicity and Complexity, Rhinestones and Diamonds

At ten thirty in the morning Andy-dam admitted one final Return Sharer to the Star Shower Sanctuary and quietly closed the heavy doors. The rustically vaulted hall smelled sharply and cleanly of varnished pine, mingling now with the musky sweetness from the banked crescent of lilies and orchids and irises fanned up behind the great wicker throne softly illuminated at the altar and of the sanctuary. Andy-dam had admitted perhaps thirty more Sharers than could be seated on the benches; at least a hundred more were clustered quietly on the sanctuary steps outside.

Andy-dam raised his hand to the control booth overhead. The lights grew dim over the benches and came up on the wicker throne. A meandering phrase of flute music grew for an instant louder then faded to silence. An amplified voice announced: "The Realized Yogananda Avatar."

A side door opened near the throne, and the Guru entered the sanctuary. There were breathy exhalations and faint moans as the

Guru approached the throne. Many of the Sharers threw back their heads in involuntary *kriyas*. The Guru paused for a moment to acknowledge the seated Sharers. He smiled faintly and sat down.

"Beloved, we welcome you this morning to this Heart Sharing at Star Shower. The Teaching I wish to offer you is about Simplicity and Complexity, but because of a certain necessary relatedness and congruence, I may offer a second Teaching on Reality.

"It is hard, isn't it"—the Guru smiled broadly—"*not* to address Reality." There was a ripple of laughter from the Sharers. "Since what else could I possibly refer to?" More laughter.

"But when we lift ourselves up out of our egoistic preoccupation with the surfaces of things and begin to commune with what is whole and complete and inalienably present, we do not always succeed. Even in deepest meditation, even in our purest humility, we can feel lost, helpless, unconnected. Hell itself has been defined as that unconnectedness. 'I maintain,' Dostoyevsky wrote, 'that hell is the inability to love.' It is the same thing. The inability to love, to be out of natural, effortless, limitless heart-communion with others and with Being itself, is what I mean when I say 'unconnected.' It is, simply, hell.

"Of course we don't want this. Nobody wants hell. But when we feel the terrible descent, we panic. And when we panic, we fall into the understandable but still hopeless trap—we try to get enormously smart about it. We try to *figure it out*. And of course, how do we do this? We do it with our brilliant, impressive *minds*. We strive mightily to analyze, to dissect, to generalize, to deduce, to induce, to reduce. We make a system, we tell that system to hold still, and then we place ourselves inside that system, and we wait for some kind of approval, some kind of satisfaction that never comes.

"It never comes, very simply, because our system isn't *the* system. Our system is egoistic clap-trap pretending to be Real when, truth be told, Reality itself doesn't behave like a system. As children we used to be told, at least I was, that the universe is so vast, and I am so small. The universe is infinite and I am tiny and finite. The real thing, the important thing, is complex, but I am hopelessly simple.

"In that scheme, all we can do is strive, in the face of so much complexity, to get a little more complex ourselves. It won't be enough. We will never be equal to the task, equal to Reality, but we feel we ought to make the gesture. And so we school ourselves. We attempt to get smarter. Some people even make it a life project— to get a little smarter. Never of course smart enough to Know and to Connect, but perhaps in some circumscribed little way, to become smarter than everyone else. Thus we become obsessed to win spelling bees or to get into Harvard or to be the first to replicate a squirrel or a baby or to rearrange energy to blow things up." Laugher. "This is smart, this is knowing, as the world reckons." More laughter.

"But this kind of smartness gets us nowhere. This kind of smartness in fact accelerates our disconnectedness, accelerates the descent into real living hell.

"At the heart of the problem is the mistaken regard for complexity and vastness. What if, my beloved friends, Reality is not complex? What if it is not vast, out of your scale, beyond you? What if you are caressing it on your palms right this second? What if you are holding it fast in the composition of your own living body? What if you are breathing it in, and, in a delightful way you can barely imagine, it is breathing you in? What if you are holding it in place—at the same time it is holding you in place? What if in order for it to be, you had to behold it and make it conscious? What if, in order for you to be conscious, it had to be?

"What if, truth be told, it was always a part of you and you were a part of it? That you were born thrillingly into it and, equally thrilling, you died into it? And that it had its very being by virtue of your living and dying?

"What if, my friends, there *is* no complexity, only simplicity? And that simplicity is just that—really simple and directly, effortlessly at hand? Because it is. *It is.* In your best heart you know it is. That is why you bother. That is why you are here. That is also why you meditate. You don't meditate in order to access the Big Complexity. You meditate in order to shed the illusion of that complexity, to grow truly simple and simply true. You meditate in order to enter the only thing there is. You meditate *instead* of winning the spelling bee and wanting the Nobel Prize and being willing to blow up the world to get it." Laughter.

"Simplicity is simple. It is simpler than the word or the idea the word represents. Even the word and the idea take some effort to understand, but the simple, true condition takes no effort to understand. It is simply a presence you affirm, affirm effortlessly. This is why you must not *work* at simplicity, like a plodding Quaker." Laughter. "Such work is the beginning of complexity. Soon you will find yourself with a system for simplicity, and perhaps you will elaborate and improve the system, and before long you will be wanting to refine your model beyond your simple friend's understanding. Maybe you will take out a patent on your approach, sell it, figure out a way to make somebody study for years to get it, and then you can give them a degree." Appreciative laughter.

"My friends—again—simplicity is simple, but it is so simple, so pure, so real that it is elusive. It is especially elusive in a world that is afraid of it and resentful of it—because it can't be hoarded and because it's a great equalizer and debunker. Everybody can have it. Everybody already has it if they can make it conscious. Everybody has it—and it is enough!

"But as I say, it is elusive. You can't *go after* it. You can't learn it or master it. You have, simply, to enter it, surrender to it, join it. You can't know all about it. You must not pretend to know. It is all right to be bewildered. Can you be bewildered without feeling anxious and impatient? Can you? Not many people can. Doing so is the beginning of simplicity, which is the beginning of all the wisdom we are going to have.

"So be bewildered! Be patiently bewildered. Be lovingly bewildered. And if you do, if you do it with all your heart, the strangest things will begin to happen. All of a sudden, one day, something ordinary, something you thought you've done a thousand times, something you thought you knew, will be for the first time Real. It will be new.

"It could be anything. It could be a song you've played a thousand times on the piano, a song you were sick of, finished with, a song you knew by heart. Then one afternoon, without a thought, you sit down idly to play it, and there is not a thought or an expectation in your head, and suddenly—there it is! The notes are like hard, brilliant gems, the chords are shimmering facets, and the progress of the song as it shapes itself is a miracle and a mystery. The mystery is that you've never heard it this way and that you have always heard it this way. And the beauty of it is its ringing simplicity, its absolute only-that-song particularity. And it is not complex. There is no complicated way to represent that perfect reality. To make it complex is to spoil it immediately.

"But it needn't be a song. It could be a phrase in that song. It could be a note. It could be a wrong note. It could be as particular as a first bite of warm toast, the reality of what toasting does to bread, or what butter does to toast, or what cheese does to buttered toast, peanut butter does for jelly, bacon does to lettuce and tomatoes. It could be what the flash of an oriole does to a clothesline on a bright morning—a clue finally to what flash and orange and oriole and morning really are. Again, it's simple. I am using words, but I am playing with you because there are no words for it, no words necessary.

"Yes, it could be the reality of toast—or a mouse skittering among your shoes in the closet, an earthworm on the sidewalk after rain, a glad surrender to being naked in the sun, puzzling over something and seeing it come right like the gathering of crystals, or seeing it come wrong. It could be the exquisite satisfaction of pissing, or cupping a beloved breast in a loving hand. It could be the glad sweet carbonated tang of Pepsi on the back of your throat.

"Like that, bang! To an open, simple heart there is one miracle—one irreplaceable miracle—after another. And one more thing, if you are not *experiencing* those things, not experiencing them but instead trying to keep track, keep score—it will all be so complex. There has never yet been a genius who could make sense of such complexity."

The Guru was exhilarated, hyper-alert. He looked out to the Sharers seated on the benches and on the floor behind. Their eyes were bright. They were rapt. Feeling a tug of discomfort at the base of his spine, the Guru adjusted his position on the satin cushions.

"And now I would like to offer a second teaching. It is related and, I am afraid, necessary.

"I have been talking to you about the Simplicity necessary in order to know Reality. Perhaps the single greatest obstacle to that necessary Simplicity is the deep, frightened desire to Have. The early Italians saw through this. They knew better. They expressed it in a little saying:

Essere non avere

To be, not to have. Having is the problem. Not real having—for as you will see, you have always had everything—but the drive, the mania to have the things around you. Think for a minute. No one who has enough, who has plenty, is bothered by having. At that moment this morning when you had all the breakfast you cared for, you did not want to have any more. What else do you have enough of? Let's say shoes. If you have enough shoes, what could drive you to want, to make mental pictures of, to move your being and displace your goods in pursuit of more shoes? Nothing. It would be pointless. We pursue having, we pursue shoes, when, like poor Mrs. Marcos, we mistake a mere thing, like a stylish pair of shoes, for Value itself. When we are frightened and unconnected and out of loving communion, we desperately form the false equation that the thing to be had equals the thing that is missing. Thus, crazily, we say: if I can have the shoes, I will be whole and happy. If I can have the car, I will be at peace. If I can have that mansion in that neighborhood, I will matter.

"As if that kind of having ever worked. As if we didn't always matter. That kind of having, beloved friends, is always *instead*. It is always compensation, never Real. Yet that kind of having drives the whole economic world, doesn't it? How, you might ask, could such an obvious, basic error become the world's standard?

"Well, I'll tell you." The Guru paused to smile, and there was laughter. "Now aren't you glad you came?" More, sustained laughter.

"The original error—the first fraud—is in the rooting of value in desire. The error is in the claim, and then the belief, that something is valuable *because* we want it. Once this primitive mistake is in play, then all the grandly authoritative Laws of Economics fall into place: the Law of Supply and Demand, the Law of Scarcity. If there is not much or enough of something, if everybody can't have it, then it's valuable! If it's scarce, it's important. If you don't have the scarce or missing thing, you are less important. If there are not enough valuables to go around, only some people can be valuable. Yes, we buy this. Literally, we buy this. And we chase after not what is beautiful and Real and intrinsically fine; we chase after what is rumored to be scarce, what somebody else might get or has gotten instead of us. Once we enter this race, we are hopelessly lost. Because the designers of the False Economy can and do keep the scarce commodities eternally scarce. And because scarcity is, in the first place, an illusion not a Reality, the economy actually runs on a succession of illusions about scarcity. It urges you first to crave, then to buy this new stylish scarcity. This new look. This spiked heel. No, this new fat heel. No, these athletic shoes. Yes, you Granny! You too must wear this scarce, irresistible shoe that the basketball stars wear. There is not enough sunlight, so you need to go to the sun, buy a piece of it, a condo, a time-share, a sleek boat that can take you there. But you can't go there in that body." Laughter. "You need this scarce, thin body, this dream body with nothing on it but the absence of fat. There are too many bodies like yours. Look at the catalogs and the magazines and take in the scarce body. Imagine having that! But there are so many interme-diate things you need to have before you can. You must have the spa, and the exercise machines, and the running gear. If you want to have the scarce body, which is almost no body at all, you must have these scarce-makers. We have made scarce—and thus desir-able—the very absences of things. We have made expensive and thus scarce and thus desirable such alluring absences as water, as food without savor, flavor or salt. You can have the scarce body if you will be salt-free, fat-free, sugar-free, food-free. The genius of Having-Economics has persuaded us that nothingness and absence must be purchased and had. In the end, because the fallacy is a perfect fallacy, we will bankrupt ourselves—willingly, even desper-ately—in our zeal to pay out all of our something for nothing.

"Again, the insanity, with all of its sad, spent personal wreckage, begins in assigning value to what is of no value. But wait, you say. Some things surely are valuable. Things in this world. Some things are at least more valuable than others. A diamond, after all, is a diamond, and a rhinestone is a rhinestone. The diamond is scarce, the rhinestone is as plentiful as we would like. A diamond is exquisitely hard, a rhinestone shatters like the glass that it is. A diamond lasts, a rhinestone breaks, dissolves, perishes.

"Beloved friends, listen to me. Diamonds are not more valuable than rhinestones. They only cost more. Imagine a tall, dark, and lovely woman, a real woman, a beauty. Let us really summon up this woman. Let's smell her clean skin and lovely scent. Let's breathe it in at the nape of her neck and in the part of her hair. Before we dress this woman, let's know the silky pleasure of the skin along her shoulders, along the delicate bones above her breasts, the smooth creamy expanse of her back. Oh, yes, this *is* a beauty, isn't she?" Muffled laughter.

"Now we will clothe her. We will drape her simply with dark velvet. We will give her elegant satin shoes. We will redden her lips and darken her lovely eyes. And now. Just before she descends the stairs to greet us, we will place a delicate diamond tiara in her hair, suspend flashing diamond earrings from her hears and clasp behind her slender neck a cascading necklace whose white and silver facets flash like fire from the base of her throat down into the beckoning cleavage of her breasts.

"Now here she comes toward us, step by step. We sense the wholeness, the power of her dark beauty. She is a particular woman, but she is carrying something of the Reality of Womanhood itself in her power, and part of it is the sparkle and flash of those diamonds. The tiara and earrings and necklace are giving back the chandelier light overhead. They are giving back the firelight and the candlelight. She is the firmament, and they, those diamonds, are its constellations.

"So how can I say those diamonds aren't valuable?" The Guru paused. He searched the eyes of the Sharers. "But I do say so. I am saying so. There is a value, a true value, in those shimmering diamonds—but! It isn't *in* the diamonds. It is in the shimmering. It is in giving back the light, in breaking up the light into tiny facets so as to celebrate, to twinkle, to tinkle like a thousand miniature bells. The beauty, the Reality, is in the twinkling, in what the diamonds *do*, not in their being diamonds. Not because they are diamonds.

"Beloved friends, do you see? Do you see what I am saying? It is not the diamonds. Because now I must tell you the whole truth. I will tell you the rest of the story. They are not diamonds. They were not diamonds in the first place. They were rhinestones. They were not merely rhinestones, as you saw. They were not rhinestones masquerading as diamonds. They where rhinestones shimmering with beauty, announcing, celebrating beauty, giving back the very light.

"Now when a rhinestone does all a diamond could do, I suppose you could say it is a diamond. But why bother to say that? What is gained? Better to say: rhinestone or diamond, it is beautiful, it is Real." The Guru paused, and for a moment his face looked troubled.

"Friends," he said abruptly, "look at me up here." He craned his neck to stare upward. "I must look very bright under these lights. These shiny cushions, this brilliant tunic. And look, these bright gold buttons. Do I sparkle? Do I shine? I am certainly a rhinestone, but am I not also a diamond?"

The Guru sat in silence for several minutes, then he rose and left the sanctuary through the side door.

7
The Sharing

The Guru told Kamala to bring no lunch, just a bottle of spring water. Alone in his darkened sleeping suite he sat heavily at the foot of the bed. He pictured the discomfort above his groin as a dark, concentrated mass, a sightless animal stirring slightly, uneasy in its sleep. The Guru depressed and unscrewed the plastic cap from the prescription bottle. He decanted four oxycontin tablets, placed them at the back of his tongue and swallowed them with bottled water.

Outside, the Sharers were rising from the long tables set with cold vegetables, hummus, fresh fruit, and juice. The air was clear and cool. Insistent midday sun prickled their faces as they made their way over the grounds. Some walked compound trails pungent with pine scent and carpeted with brown needles. Some found a quiet spot on the bank of the stream and meditated to the hiss and gurgle of the water rushing over the rocks. Others gathered into impromptu clusters for directed yoga.

Later the collective sense of unhurried anticipation was heightened perceptibly as the visitors began climbing the paths, up to the granite terrace of the Ridge Past Caring for the pre-Sharing vigil. The Ridge Past Caring was a rocky clearing on the crest of a hillock at the far end of the Great Meadow. The clearing looked out over green acres of meadow and the compound Pavilion.

At no set hour, but when the afternoon light gave way to evening light, strains of amplified music were piped over the grounds, softly, hardly audible at first, flute and sitar and wordless chants of a treble choir. As the Sharers made their way down from the ridge to the Pavilion at the center of the Great Meadow, the music grew gradually louder, and the percussive force of the bass notes could be heard and felt. Now the voices were robust, male voices, Hymns to Yogananda.

The Sharers fanned out around the oval thrust of the Pavilion stage, and the chanting of Astral Pain became driving and urgent, emanating not, it seemed, from the speakers recessed in the branches of the aspens lining the meadow, but from the leaves and trees themselves.

The sun is the light

And the light is the eye

And the eye opens bright

To the all of the sky

Yo-ga-nan-da o-pen me

Yo-ga-nan-da o-pen me

Yo-ga-nan-da o-pen me

Yo-ga-nan-da o-pen me

The Sharers were aware of one another and oblivious of one another, together and alone. Eyes were closed, arms raised. Shoulders and hips moved with the pulsing cadence. Some were singing, others silently mouthing the refrain. The Sharers felt they were singing Astral Pain, that Astral Pain was singing through them. The music seemed to grow louder, louder than music, louder than sound, and some of the Sharers of grew rigid and trembled. Heads were thrown back in jarring kriyas, and the Sharers felt the helpless constricting and glugging in their throats and a taste like dark blood, like the sea.

The air was gusting now, slapping the bright cloth of saris and sarongs against belly and thigh. The sky was still glass blue, but the radiance had withdrawn, creating a feeling of frozenness, of time holding its breath. For many Sharers this was too much, and they convulsed in sobs, straining to fill their lungs, to cry out.

And then the Guru was there, first on the Pavilion stage and then down among them on the grass. They had seen him arrive, and they had not seen. Late afternoon sun made fiery spangles on the gold and scarlet sheen of his tunic. The Guru was a poster, a photograph, a sculpture of himself, but there he was too in his living skin, in the shadowy planes of his face, little wisps of grey and white hair at the back of his neck. There was his girth, the grey-pink of his pallor, the striding fullness of his arms and legs as he approached—the white simple slabs of his sandaled feet.

Reflexively, reverently, the Sharers parted a path before the Guru. The air was charged with the pulsing drone of a single musical tone.

The Guru heard the roar in his ears. He saw the shimmering wash of colors and forms part before him as he advanced. He felt his force, his heaviness, felt it moving forward into the Sharers. He stopped, and the Sharers fell back leaving him encircled. He wheeled slowly, meeting their eyes. He felt the eruption of his smile. He felt it like a great sun rising up from his throat into the center of his skull. He heard the sharp clout of his own laughter rise into the meadow air. The Guru raised his arms, and the Sharers roared, wept, dropped to their knees.

The Guru walked on. Deep, poisonous emanations rose from his gut up into his head. He breathed deeply, and for a moment the dizziness enveloped him, darkening his vision, and then he felt it dissolve into the familiar pleasure.

Again the grassy path opened up before his feet, and he was moving among the sharers. Each now was wonderfully particular, the shine and fall of their hair, the telling set of their faces.

The air between their bodies and his was charged, excited with their releases. A succession of still images—the line of a mouth, a pointed chin, the amplitude of breasts—carried an unguarded finality, the wholeness of each Sharer.

The Guru paused. He stood face to face with Gannett Witherspoon. Gannett Witherspoon's matted hair was streaked with grey, and his face was moist with perspiration. His eyes met the Guru's, and there was no resistance. The Guru took in Gannett Witherspoon's bowed shoulders, his white cotton shirt, sleeves rolled tightly to the elbow, white trousers, white canvas shoes. The Guru saw that Gannett Witherspoon was fully realized. The Guru placed his hands heavily on Gannett Witherspoon's shoulders and said, "You are wearing white for me."

Gannett Witherspoon smiled. "Yes."

The Guru embraced Gannett Witherspoon, drawing his slender form into himself, enveloping him.

The Guru moved on among the Sharers. They raised their arms at his approach. Some of them dropped to their knees. They crouched low, bowed their heads before him. There, three or four persons back from the path, a drooping moustache and strong stubbled chin captured the Guru's gaze. The chin was familiar, wonderfully complete, and the Guru looked into the wide, helpless eyes of Farr Rockaway. Farr Rockaway cried out, and the sound of his cry blended into the hum of the Sharers, into the pulsing musical tone.

Farr Rockaway thrust an arm over the shoulders of the Sharers in front of him and opened his hand to the Guru. The Guru smiled, looked hard into Farr Rockaway's eyes, and clasped his fingers into his palm.

There were shouts, releases of pleasure, eruptions of wordless song. The Guru let the particulars coalesce into unity, let the faces become a face, the bodies a body. For an instant the darkly recessed eyes and mustache and chin of Farr Rockaway rested like a bright orb on the whitely clad body of Gannett Witherspoon. Then the Guru was walking on, moving faster, letting the faces dissolve into adjacent faces. Without stopping, the Guru passed the grinning figure of Danny Katz, balding now, his mouth working, the words trailing like butterflies in the Guru's wake.

The Guru turned sharply, penetrating the massed Sharers before they could open up a pathway. His arms, his hips brushed coolly against their bodies. There were excited hums. There was the pulsing musical tone.

The Guru stood before Trish Triester. She opened her arms to the Guru, and they held each other. They rocked slightly from foot to foot. The Guru felt the comfortable fullness of her breasts at his breast, felt it penetrate his ribs and enter his fullness.

"You are love," the Guru said into her ear.

"Yes," Trish Triester said. "Always."

The Guru knew that he was walking, moving among the Sharers, but for a time he did not see them. He was aware of the din, but he did not hear it. He was looking within. He felt suspended in a dark medium, like deep water.

Then the din was fresh, raucous in his ears, and he was moving, very quickly now, past the particulars, past the faces. He was approaching the periphery of the Sharers, the end of them. The pathway opened onto the wide meadow. The grassy expanse before him glowed emerald green in the declining light.

Just before departing the Sharers, the Guru stopped still and turned to the man standing just outside the circle. He wore a vee-neck sweater over a clean white shirt. He withdrew his hands from the pockets of his pants and looked up into the Guru's eyes. The Guru moved in close to him, took both of his hands.

"Forrester," the Guru said.

"Yes."

The Guru smiled. "We went back a long way."

"Yes."

The Guru saw Forrester's face soften, felt him surrender.

The Guru left the Sharers behind him and continued out into the open meadow in the direction of the Ridge Past Caring. He did not see or hear the Sharers quietly disperse. The swollen ridge ahead was a brilliant yellow green.

The Guru felt something beckoning in the bright mounded form, sensed beneath its grassy bank a pillowed softness, and the softness called him. A gust flattened the grasses before his feet, and the sound was like a voice, and the cushioned bulge of the ridge was a welcome presence against the Guru's face and neck and breast. It gathered him in, as he had gathered in the fullness of Trish Triester, and he knew that it was Granny Mueller, and that she was again, forever, gathering him into her.

The Guru stood back on his heels and assumed the glowing ridge, Granny Mueller, into his knowing.

The Guru offered an all-being prayer for what he was given.

IV

The Guru Returns
To the Sea

1
Heart's Rest

On the return journey to Heart's Rest Cay, the Guru was more than withdrawn, he was unreachable.

Andy-dam had been reluctant to stay behind when the Guru asked that he oversee the winter preparations at Star Shower. The Guru looked to him vacant and spent, and Andy-dam was uneasy.

"Are you sure I can't help you on the trip? I am happy to go with you. I would *like* to help."

"No," the Guru had said. "But you are kind to offer. You must help me here."

Curtis Forbes, too, was concerned when the Guru informed him that he would like to return to Heart's Rest with Kamala alone. The Guru asked Curtis Forbes to see that his prescription was renewed.

"Tell me how you are feeling," Curtis Forbes had said.

The Guru smiled. "I am always the same."

"I meant your body, the discomfort."

"I know what you mean. Curtis, I have to return."

"Do you have to go alone?"

"You always return alone." The Guru smiled again. "And there will be Kamala."

The Guru looked to Curtis Forbes as if he had departed already.

The Guru adjusted his position against the pillows bunched along the headboard of the bed. With effort he drew his knees up close to his chest. White slivers of sunlight flashed between the slats of the drawn blinds. The Guru sensed the radiance, the force of the morning light on the terrace garden outside. He could hear the plip-plop of the fountain in the bathing pool.

The Guru could not remember awakening. The stillness in the suite seemed continuous with the stillness of the flights, the stale, sour compression between Denver and Miami, the tinny, buzzing passage from Miami to Heart's Rest. He had given himself up to the medicine, said a prayerful yes to the capsules. Kamala had stopped trying to speak to him. She had been there, close at his side, and not there.

In the plane he felt himself gathered like a crescent of gauzy light over the glowing coals of his distress. From the untroubled light of this crescent, he could monitor precisely the slow aches, the occasional searing spikes of pain below.

The Guru lowered his head down against his knees. He felt and did not feel the slow rising and falling of pressure in his core, the clench and release, like breaking waves. *It has become*, he realized, *what I am.*

2

Kamala in the Fountain

The Guru turned to the night table and filled a glass with spring water. He unscrewed the plastic cap from the prescription bottle and emptied the capsules onto the pillow next to him. He sat up and fixed his gaze on the slits of radiance escaping from the blinds. He swallowed back the capsules until he had drunk all of the water in the glass.

The Guru breathed deeply, stretched his legs out before him, and rose heavily from the bed. He felt the weight of his belly, all of his girth, straining downward toward the floor, as if it wanted to fall free of his skeleton. For an instant the Guru teetered on his feet, uncertain of his balance.

The Guru knew he must move, go out. He opened the sash of his robe and let it slide from his shoulders. He felt the silk caress his nakedness as it fell. He sensed in his peripheral vision the progress of his grey bulk in the mirrors as he moved to the door to the terrace.

Outside the Guru stood blinking in the brilliant light. Irides-cent hummingbirds made quick jittery arcs in the bougainvillea. The morning sun was insistent on the crown of his head and on the back of his neck. The terra cotta tiles were hot beneath his feet.

The Guru looked past the fountain, past the strip of green lawn, past the white sand of the beach to the sea. He saw the aquamarine of the sandy shallows darken to a deep purple blue as it approached the horizon. The tiles were burning the soles of his feet, and he moved to the fountain. At the center of the circular pool a jet of water erupted from behind the wings of two opposed stone angels and fell like raindrops onto the sparkling surface. The Guru stepped into the pool and felt the tepid coolness rise up over his knees.

Something insistent—a memory—seemed to be on the brink of arrival, but it would not come. The Guru caught a reflection of his image in the glass of the terrace door. The mass of his upper body looked pale and livid in contrast to the greenery, the flowers, the azure sky. The Guru was at once fascinated and repulsed by his naked image, which he could see now with photographic clarity.

Then the Guru remembered Kamala in the fountain. It was the morning after they had come, years ago, to Heart's Rest to inspect the renovations: the restoration of the old villa, the landscaping of the terrace and garden beach, the installation of the fountain. The buildings, the island itself, had seemed to be made new. The compound when they arrived was brightly appointed, spotlessly clean. Freshly cut flowers had been set out in every room. It was exactly as the Guru had pictured it would be.

That morning the Guru had walked out onto the sun-blanched terrace and greeted Kamala who was sunning naked on the ledge of the fountain. The honey gold expanse of her long legs and belly, the slightly paler rise of her resting breasts, were gladdeningly continuous with the flowers, the new orange tiles, the arc of the sea beyond, with the busy, living air.

The Guru joined Kamala at the fountain. He had closed his eyes as she smoothed sun lotion smelling of chocolate and coconut over his arms and legs, belly and back, already browned from the summer at the Star Shower and the Maui Retreat.

The Guru could smell the chocolate and coconut. He could see and hear, even in this suffocating air, the plop and fizz of the new fountain.

All that morning, all that day the Guru and Kamala had played and pleasured one another in the shallow water of the fountain. Kamala had reclined on her back and with his palm lightly at the base of her spine, the Guru had guided her silently in orbit after orbit around the stone angels. They had taken each other in and out of the water, standing, seated, half-submerged, kissed, touched, Kamala had said, like children. *Like the first children,* the Guru had said. They had lain back together in the water, necks propped against the lip of the fountain, faces inclined up into the sun. They had stood up together and embraced, and the Guru saw the reflection of their combined forms in the glass of the terrace door. They were one golden skinned figure, pleasingly related. Water was beaded on their backs, he remembered, and it had been beautiful. It had been an all-being prayer, all that day in the fountain.

The Guru turned away and then looked back once more at the reflection of his pale girth in the glass of the door. There was a jarring sensation, like a harsh handclap just behind his eyes. *I do not belong.*

The Guru stepped heavily out of the fountain. The heat, the close air seemed to press in against his temples, narrowing his field of vision. He felt himself sink into the depths of his belly and for an instant he seemed to taste, to breathe in the putrification of his own distress. He wondered if he could move, if he could continue to stand.

The Guru stepped flat footedly over the hot tiles to the prickly grass, then over the sand until he splashed into the shallows. He closed his eyes to a clout of white sunlight on the water, and he felt himself fall backwards.

The Guru reclined back on his elbows in the shallows. Ripples rose and fell under his chin, and the water was cooler than the fountain, rising and falling, until it was not cooler.

The Guru rolled over onto his hands and knees. He raised back his head and eyed the open horizon. He drew in his breath and launched himself out over the surface of the water. He opened his eyes to the dappled shadows on the sandy bottom, folding back into themselves in the wavery aquamarine. Then the sandy bottom, the water, the light itself drew back through his eyes into the center of his skull, and with another sharp clap there was black silence.

The Guru opened his eyes. He was lying out over the surface of the bright water, rising and falling with it, seeing and not seeing.